NASHVILLE | BOOK TEN | NOT WITHOUT YOU

NASHVILLE | BOOK TEN | NOT WITHOUT YOU

INGLATH COOPER

Contents

Copyright   vii
Books by Inglath Cooper   viii
Reviews   ix
*   xi

CeCe   2
CeCe   6
Holden   11
CeCe   14
CeCe   16
Holden   19
CeCe   22
Holden   24
CeCe   26
Holden   29
Holden   30
CeCe   34
Holden   36
CeCe   37
Holden   39
CeCe   41

CeCe   44
CeCe   46
Holden   48
CeCe   49
Holden   52
CeCe   53
Holden   56
CeCe   59
Holden   62
CeCe   66
Holden   69
CeCe   73
Holden   75
CeCe   76
Holden   77
Holden   82
CeCe   84
CeCe   86
Holden   87
CeCe   89
Holden   92

Thirteen Months Later   95
CeCe   96
Holden   101
CeCe   103
Holden   105
CeCe   106
Holden   108
CeCe   109
Holden   110
CeCe   112

Holden	114
CeCe	115
CeCe	116
Holden	117
Holden	118
CeCe	120
CeCe	121
Holden	124
CeCe	128
Holden	129
Dear Reader	131
Get in Touch with Inglath Cooper	132
Books By Inglath Cooper	133
About Inglath Cooper	134

Copyright

Books by Inglath Cooper

Swerve

The Heart That Breaks

My Italian Lover

Fences – Book Three – Smith Mountain Lake Series

Dragonfly Summer – Book Two – Smith Mountain Lake Series

Blue Wide Sky – Book One – Smith Mountain Lake Series

That Month in Tuscany

And Then You Loved Me

Down a Country Road

Good Guys Love Dogs

Truths and Roses

Nashville – Part Ten – Not Without You

Nashville – Book Nine – You, Me and a Palm Tree

Nashville – Book Eight – R U Serious

Nashville – Book Seven – Commit

Nashville – Book Six – Sweet Tea and Me

Nashville – Book Five – Amazed

Nashville – Book Four – Pleasure in the Rain

Nashville – Book Three – What We Feel

Nashville – Book Two – Hammer and a Song

Nashville – Book One – Ready to Reach

On Angel's Wings

A Gift of Grace

RITA® Award Winner John Riley's Girl

A Woman With Secrets

Unfinished Business

A Woman Like Annie

The Lost Daughter of Pigeon Hollow

A Year and a Day

Reviews

"If you like your romance in New Adult flavor, with plenty of ups and downs, oh-my, oh-yes, oh-no, love at first sight, trouble, happiness, difficulty, and follow-your-dreams, look no further than extraordinary prolific author Inglath Cooper. Ms. Cooper understands that the romance genre deserves good writing, great characterization, and true-to-life settings and situations, no matter the setting. I recommend you turn off the phone and ignore the doorbell, as you're not going to want to miss a moment of this saga of the girl who headed for Nashville with only a guitar, a hound, and a Dream in her heart." – **Mallory Heart Reviews**

"Truths and Roses . . . so sweet and adorable, I didn't want to stop reading it. I could have put it down and picked it up again in the morning, but I didn't want to." – **Kirkusreviews.com**

On Truths and Roses: "I adored this book...what romance should be, entwined with real feelings, real life and roses blooming. Hats off to the author, best book I have read in a while." – **Rachel Dove, FrustratedYukkyMommyBlog**

"I am a sucker for sweet love stories! This is definitely one of those! It was a very easy, well written, book. It was easy to follow, detailed, and didn't leave me hanging without answers." – **www.layfieldbaby.blogspot.com**

"I don't give it often, but I am giving it here – the sacred 10. Why? Inglath Cooper's A GIFT OF GRACE mesmerized me; I consumed it in one sitting. When I turned the last page, it was three in the morning." – **MaryGrace Meloche, Contemporary Romance Writers**

5 Blue Ribbon Rating! ". . .More a work of art than a story. . .Tragedies affect entire families as well as close loved ones, and this story portrays that beautifully as well as giving the reader hope

that somewhere out there is A GIFT OF GRACE for all of us."
— **Chrissy Dionne, Romance Junkies 5 Stars**

"A warm contemporary family drama, starring likable people coping with tragedy and triumph." 4 1/2 Stars. — **Harriet Klausner**

"A GIFT OF GRACE is a beautiful, intense, and superbly written novel about grief and letting go, second chances and coming alive again after devastating adversity. Warning!! A GIFT OF GRACE is a three-hanky read…better make that a BIG box of tissues read! Wowsers, I haven't cried so much while reading a book in a long long time…Ms. Cooper's skill makes A GIFT OF GRACE totally believable, totally absorbing…and makes Laney Tucker vibrantly alive. This book will get into your heart and it will NOT let go. A GIFT OF GRACE is simply stunning in every way—brava, Ms. Cooper! Highly, highly recommended!" – **4 1/2 Hearts — Romance Readers Connection**

"…A WOMAN WITH SECRETS…a powerful love story laced with treachery, deceit and old wounds that will not heal…enchanting tale…weaved with passion, humor, broken hearts and a commanding love that will have your heart soaring and cheering for a happily-ever-after love. Kate is strong-willed, passionate and suffers a bruised heart. Cole is sexy, stubborn and also suffers a bruised heart…gripping plot. I look forward to reading more of Ms. Cooper's work!" – **www.freshfiction.com**

★

A Contemporary Romance set in the heart of country music. Nashville.

Sometimes, it's hard to know what we have until we realize we might lose it. CeCe and Holden Ashford have seen many of their dreams come true. Among them, a successful career in Nashville and finding the love of a lifetime in each other. But when CeCe makes the decision to accompany fellow country music star Jacob Bartley to an orphanage in Belize, everything she and Holden have come to take for granted will no longer be a given. Will an unexpected turn in events prevent them from ever finding their way back together again?

***

CeCe

I GUESS EVERYONE must have some kind of mental image of what an orphanage would be like.

Growing up, I remember reading books about children who lived in one, and, for the most part, it always seemed like they had extra magical lives with adventure after adventure and no parents to tell them what to do.

And so, somehow, I am not at all prepared for the reality of this one. Of so many young children, toddlers, and infants, whose physical and emotional needs are so minimally met.

Jacob and I arrived at the orphanage in Belize at just after ten this morning. The director and three of the caretakers gave him a king's greeting, and I was surprised by his obvious effort to downplay it. When he introduced me to each of them, I could see how appreciative they were of my interest in their efforts.

The director asks to meet with Jacob in her office, so I watch two of the caretakers in the toddler room as they hand out snacks of plain white crackers and small paper cups of water.

There are at least fifty children in the room. They sit at tables of six or eight, their hands folded neatly in their laps. There are no smiles on their faces, no excited fidgeting. They all wait until every child has received his or her snack, and at the caretaker's nod, they begin eating their three small crackers.

I watch them, too surprised to know what to think. The surprise quickly turns to something else, and tears spring up, spilling down my face. I turn away, but not before the caretaker notices my crying.

I walk to the window at the center of the room, my arms folded across my chest. I bite my lip hard to stop the flow of tears. The last thing these children need is to see me feeling sorry for them.

Someone touches my shoulder, and I glance around to see the

caretaker studying me with a sympathetic look on her face. "It is hard when you first come here," she says in extremely good English. "They do not have what other children who have families have, but they have enough. And they are grateful for it."

I hear her words, recognize her sincerity, but I can't agree with her. It's not natural for children to sit so quietly, wait so patiently. I have the feeling that they have grown used to not having enough.

And that's so wrong. They should have milk on their faces. Their laughter and giggles should fill the room, not silence.

I think of the kindergarten classroom Holden and I visited not long ago in Nashville. How vibrant and alive with joy the children had been, singing along with me while Holden played the guitar. Their happiness had been a nearly tangible thing, and I can't help but think that is something these children do not have.

"We do the best we can with what we have," the caretaker says, and I can hear in her voice that she truly believes this. Am I arrogant to think that the care the children receive isn't good enough? That they deserve more and should have more?

It doesn't feel like arrogance though. I just can't imagine that they will spend their childhood not knowing joy and the certainty that they won't go to bed hungry.

Jacob returns from his meeting with the director just then. I glance around to see the worried look on his face.

"What is it?" I ask.

"Giovanna. That's the baby's name. They had to take her to the hospital this morning. They're afraid she might have pneumonia."

"Oh, no," I say, suddenly stricken with fear for her.

"They're waiting to hear from the doctors there."

"It's so unfair," I say, a little stunned by the news. "She already has so much to overcome."

"Let's think positively," he says. "She'll be okay." He puts a hand on my shoulder and squeezes once. I look up at him, unable to hide my sadness.

"I hope you're right," I say.

"This place is a little overwhelming," he says, his voice low. "The first time I came here, I could only think about how unfair it is for the children not to be in a family, not to have a regular life."

"How did you get past that?" I ask, shaking my head.

"I didn't completely. I just tried to focus on how I could make things here better. When I was a little younger, I think I believed monumental change could be accomplished in one fell swoop if a person had enough determination. But I don't think that anymore. Things rarely get changed overnight. And I guess I've come to realize that making something better is just as worthwhile a goal."

"I know you're right," I say. "It's just—"

"Hard," he finishes, putting his arm around my shoulders and hugging me to him. "Most people don't have the courage to see things they don't think they can handle. It's easier not to look. But you're not doing that. You're here. And you're going to make a difference."

I step out of his embrace, feeling suddenly uncomfortable with his touch. I think about Holden, the way he hadn't met my gaze when I'd left the house last night, the fact that he hasn't replied to any of my texts since then. I know he has a right to worry about Jacob's intentions, but my intentions are to do something worthwhile for these children, and that is all.

Jacob gives me a look of apology and says, "Sorry, CeCe. I didn't mean to step over the line."

And now I feel petty, as if I'm accusing him of something he didn't mean. "No, I'm the one who's sorry. I'm just a little . . . surprised, I guess."

"I know the first difference we can make," he says, a smile breaking across his really too-good-looking face.

"What's that?"

"We have about a thousand boxes of animal cookies in the van. I know we can improve on those pitiful crackers they just had."

"That's awesome," I say, suddenly revived by the thought of them each getting their own box.

We go outside to the van where the driver opens up the back for us.

Jacob pulls out one of the big boxes and begins filling a large canvas tote with little red boxes of animal cookies.

I fill another, and we head back in to hand them out. The children are still at their tables. Jacob checks with the caretaker to make sure it's okay, and then begins pulling them from the bag and placing a box in front of each child.

Without exception, every boy and girl in the room looks as if they have been given something priceless. They open the tops and stick their little hands inside the boxes to pull out a single cookie, looking at it with such pleasure and gratitude that I am again overcome with the desire to do whatever I can to make their lives better. Their happiness is so gratifying that I can see why Jacob comes back again and again.

It's one thing to give people something they enjoy, like the music we play. I still feel so grateful to perform and see that people like what we do.

But this . . . this feels completely different. Giving something so simple to a child who has nothing and seeing the happiness it brings to them.

Like Jacob, I don't think I could ever grow tired of seeing it for myself.

♪

CeCe

THE VAN IS completely packed with boxes.

Once the children finish their cookies and are taken outside to play, Jacob and I begin unloading the boxes and bringing them inside the orphanage building.

It's kind of like we're playing Santa Claus, and it feels incredibly good to be a part of it.

I'm amazed by what each box contains. There are medical goods: thermometers, over-the-counter medications for fever and upset stomach. Clothes for toddlers, pink dresses for girls, football jerseys for the boys. And toys, just plain fun ones like NERF footballs and Play-Doh. And also LeapFrog learning pads that will be a wonderful tool for helping the children learn to read.

"How did you manage to get all this?" I ask, looking at Jacob in amazement.

"Beg, borrow, and steal?" he says with a grin.

"Did not."

"Didn't have to," he admits. "I have this theory that most people actually want to be generous when it's made easy for them to be so. Most of this I was able to get just by making phone calls and asking. And I like to throw out the names of donors during my concerts as a way of thanking them."

"That's really smart," I say.

He shrugs, as if I've made him uncomfortable. "Learned a few things growing up in the country. Mostly that people need to be willing to help one another out."

I pull back the lid on another box, this one full of diapers and baby wipes.

Jacob glances inside and says, "When I first came here, they were taking the babies out of diapers at one year old and starting them on the potty."

"But that's so young—"

"I know," he says with a nod. "They simply didn't have enough diapers to go around."

"And now they do."

"Now they do," he says.

"You've done an amazing thing, Jacob," I say.

He looks off at the horizon where a small plane is a dot against the sky. "Didn't someone say you get back in this world what you give out?"

"Do you really think most people subscribe to that theory?"

"Actually, I do."

I tear open the lid of another box. "I sound jaded, don't I?"

He gives me a long look, and I can feel the sympathy in his gaze when he says, "You've experienced some tough stuff, CeCe. Things that would understandably make a person jaded."

"But that's not who I want to be."

"Then you don't have to. In the end, we're left with the choice."

"You're not old enough to be so wise."

He laughs a little. "My mama's word for it was hard-headed."

I smile. "Mine too."

"Something else we have in common."

"There you go again," I chastise.

"It's the hard-headed thing."

I can't help but smile. He's wrong to flirt. I'm wrong to give him any leeway at all, but most of the time, he seems harmless. And I like his lightness. The way he looks at the world with an if not this, then that kind of philosophy. I realize how serious Holden and I have become. How weighted I feel by the things that have happened to us.

Guilt instantly strangles me. I turn my back to Jacob and reach inside the van for another box. I feel his hands at my waist, reach back to push them away. But he's strong and turns me to face him. I look up, surprised by the caring in his eyes.

"Hey," he says. "There's nothing wrong with the two of us being friends. Is there?"

"Jacob—"

"I'm not going to deny it," he interrupts. "I want more. And I'll willingly take whatever you'll give me."

"You're a good guy," I say. "So why are you doing this?"

"What?" he asks, his voice velvet soft.

"I'm married."

"You are."

"A good guy doesn't cross that line."

"And I won't. Unless you ask me to."

"I'm not going to."

"People change, CeCe. Things change."

"Some things don't."

"You and Holden, for example."

I nod.

He's silent for a few seconds, and then, "This is a hard business we're in. You start out thinking you know exactly who you are, what you're about, where you'll end up. But somehow, even though you try not to be affected by it all, it ends up happening anyway."

"You're talking about your marriage?"

"Yeah," he says.

"I know what I have, Jacob."

"I thought I did too."

"Stop."

"What?"

"Trying to make me doubt."

"I'm not. I'm just sharing my experience."

"We're not the same."

He studies me for several long seconds, picks up a box and walks toward the orphanage building. And even though he's not facing me, his voice carries clearly when he says, "Maybe more so than you think."

♪

FOR THE REST of the day, Jacob and I work at putting away the donations. It's nearly four by the time we're finished, and then we spend an hour or so with him making a list of things that need to be done, painting, window repairs, ceiling tiles that need to be replaced.

Once he's done, we walk to the director's office. Jacob knocks, and she tells us to come in.

"I was just getting ready to look for you," she says. "I'm afraid the doctor wants to keep Giovanna in the hospital tonight. He will let us know of her progress in the morning. I'm sorry if this will disrupt your plans."

"Don't worry," Jacob reassures her. "Will we still meet with the officials tomorrow?"

"I think it is better if we wait to see the prognosis for little Giovanna. If they believe she is sick, they will never agree to let her go. It is possible for you to stay a few days, I hope?" she asks.

Jacob looks at me, and I realize our plans have now been changed significantly. I think about Holden and how I will explain this to him. At the same time, I've come this far and I can't turn my back on this little girl now.

"It's fine," I say.

"We'll wait then," he tells the older woman. "We'll make use of our time by taking care of some of the things on this list." He waves the sheet of paper with his notes on it. Think we can get that same crew of guys I worked with last time to help out?"

"I am sure of it," the director says, smiling at him. "It is as I told you before. You are an angel from heaven, dear Jacob."

"If she only knew, right, CeCe?" Jacob says, looking at me with a grin.

"Oh, I have read the tabloids online," the woman says. "I know all about your dalliances. Someday, I just might tell them about the real you."

"Well, someone needs to set them straight," he teases.

"Thank you, CeCe," she says, looking at me now, "for coming here to help Giovanna. I cannot tell you how grateful I am."

"It's my pleasure," I say, somehow surprised by her sincerity. She seems so obviously dedicated to her job and providing for the children here that I cannot imagine how frustrating it must be for her when help is not readily available.

"Can you make the call about the work tomorrow?" Jacob asks.

"Of course."

"We will see you in the morning then," he says.

"Have a good night," she calls out as we leave her office.

Outside, the van driver is waiting for us, sliding open the door as we climb inside. He pulls away from the orphanage, and I can't help glancing back.

"It doesn't take long, does it?" Jacob says, looking at me with a warm smile.

"I want to take them all home with me," I say.

"I know. I feel that way every time I'm here."

I lean my head against the seat, staring out at the darkening sky beyond the van window.

"It's been a long day," he says. "We'll have a great dinner and get some sleep. Sound good?"

"Where are we staying?" I ask, realizing I have left all of this up to him.

"It's called the Cayo Espanto. It's on a small island about twenty minutes away. We'll get there by boat. I promise you it'll be worth it."

"I don't need anywhere fancy, Jacob."

"It's the least I can do for bringing you all this way," he says.

I start to argue, but realize I'm too tired to do so. I pull my phone from my purse, glance at my text messages. There's one from mama, checking to see if I'm okay.

There are none from Holden.

♪

Holden

I'M DISCOVERING THAT trying to act normal when nothing is normal is not something I'm good at.

After waking up with my arm across CeCe's empty side of the bed, I started the morning at the gym, hoping to take some of my frustration out on the rack of weights in a lesser-used part of the club. I have no desire to be around anyone because I don't see the point of inflicting my misery on any other living being.

Even Hank and Patsy seemed to sense the black cloud around me, and other than coming into the kitchen for their breakfast, they both left me and my mood to myself.

I actually turned my phone off at some point because I couldn't quit glancing at the screen every ten seconds to check for a text from CeCe. With the way I'd closed her out before she left, I don't know why I would expect her to reach out.

It's after dinnertime, and I'm in the kitchen making a sandwich I have no interest in eating when the doorbell rings. I walk to the window, spot Thomas's truck in the driveway and open the door to find him glaring at me.

"What the hell, man?"

"What?" I ask, still holding the sandwich in my hand.

"Why aren't you answering your phone?"

I shrug and turn back toward the kitchen. "I turned it off. People do that."

"You don't," he says, following me in.

"People change," I throw back.

"You mean people pout," he says, opening the refrigerator and pulling out a beer, then handing me one.

I put down the sandwich, realizing I'd much rather have the beer. "I'm not pouting."

"Yeah, you are."

"I'm not five."

"Well, you're kind of acting like it."

I take a sip of the beer and give him a long look. "Like you'd be in Blissville if Lila went to Belize with Jacob Bartley."

"I'd have gone with her. That was your mistake."

The dart stings with truth. "Why do you always have to be right?"

"Why do you always have to be stubborn?"

"I didn't want her to go."

"I know."

"She knew."

"But she wanted to. Maybe she needed to."

"Sometimes, in a marriage, you don't always get to do what you need or want to do."

"Been listening to Dr. Phil again?"

I give him a glare, and he backs down.

"All right, I probably would have been pissed too. But here you are. The situation has happened, and you can either be a complete ass and seriously mess up what you and CeCe have. Or you can rise above it and be here for her when she gets back. Which is when?"

"Sometime tomorrow."

"That'll be here before you know it. Man, you gotta trust in what you two have. We're all going to get tested now and then. Consider this your test."

"I hate tests."

"It seems to me you've got a shot at making an A on this one. Be cool, and you're the one she comes back to."

"I wish I were as sure of that as you are."

Hank Junior walks into the kitchen, wagging his tail as he walks over to greet Thomas. Thomas rubs his head. "Hank knows she'll be back. Don't you, boy?"

Hank wags his tail harder, clearly aware of who Thomas is talking about.

"So the reason I was trying to call you is Lila and I are going out to dinner. You're going with us."

"I'd be terrible company," I say. "You two go and have fun."

"We're not going without you," Thomas says, getting up from the bar stool. "Get dressed, and I'll be back in forty-five minutes."

"Anybody ever tell you you're too damn bossy?" I ask.

"A time or two," he throws back on the way out of the kitchen.

"Where are we going?"

"Lila said somewhere swanky so look the part."

And before I can argue any further, he's out the door.

♪

CeCe

A PRIVATE CHARTER boat takes us to the small island and Cayo Espanto where we'll be staying. It's beautiful, lights throwing shadows across the beach as we pull up to the dock. It's nearly dark, and I realize that I am both starving and exhausted.

A golf cart is waiting for us at the end of the pier. The driver greets us with a smile, taking the two bags we're carrying.

"You can get whatever you need at the hotel," Jacob says.

"At least I have my toothbrush," I say.

"There are boutiques where you can get some clothes and pajamas."

"You've stayed here before?" I ask, as the golf cart navigates a winding path lined with low lights.

"It's an indulgence," he says. "I admit I felt guilty at first, staying at such a nice place when I'm working at an orphanage during the day. But it was actually Mrs. Castellanos's suggestion because of the security here. She's afraid I'll be kidnapped and held for ransom."

I feel a little jolt of alarm. "Do things like that actually happen here?"

He shrugs, unconcerned. "I think she's just being overprotective."

"She's very fond of you. That's obvious."

He meets my gaze when he says, "I think I'm a nicer person here."

"What do you mean?"

"Without all the fan stuff. You have to admit, it starts to get easy to believe your own press."

"I think I'm still in the it-can-all-go-away-any-day phase."

"You're right to stay humble. Because it could go away like that," he says, snapping his fingers, "for any of us at any time."

"My goal is to enjoy it while it lasts. Being able to sing for a living is still kind of unbelievable to me."

"I can't disagree with that. You know, I just don't want to get surprised by the day when it changes. I want to know that I've put other things in my life that will still make me want to get up every morning."

"Like what you do here?"

"Yeah, I guess so," he says.

"You know what I think?"

"What?" he asks, looking at me directly.

"I think you want the world to believe you're a badass when you're actually not."

"Did you say badass?"

I laugh. I can't help it. "I did."

"And I thought I had you fooled."

"Not anymore," I say.

♪

CeCe

MY ROOM IS like something out of a Caribbean fantasy.

It's right on the beach, and with the glass pane doors open, I can hear the constant lap and pull of the ocean just outside.

An enormous bed sits in the middle of the room, draped in a sea blue sheer canopy. The bathroom is a marble masterpiece, and I slip out of my clothes and into the oversize tub with a sigh of appreciation.

I soak in lavender bath salts until my muscles lose their tired ache. I reach for my phone on the side of the tub and call Holden. My stomach flutters with nerves while it rings and then goes to voice mail.

I wanted to tell him about the change in plans myself, but since I can't reach him, I type in a text.

Hey,

Just tried to call. Everything is fine, but we might be staying in Belize for a few days. Giovanna, the baby we were hopefully bringing back, has been admitted to the hospital. She might have pneumonia. I will let you know what we learn tomorrow. I miss you.

I put the phone down, sitting up in the tub and wrapping my arms around my knees. I feel guilty and worried and sick about the conflict between Holden and me. If we could just talk, I could reassure him that he has nothing to worry about.

The phone rings. My heart leaps just as I see Jacob's name flash on the screen.

"Hey," I say.

"Room okay?" he asks.

16

"Incredible."

"Good. How about some dinner?"

"Ah, I don't have anything to wear."

"Funny you should mention that. I just had something sent up."

"Jacob, you didn't have to do that."

"I'm pretty good at guessing sizes."

"Is that from helping girls on or off with their clothes?"

He laughs and says, "Ouch."

"I'm sorry. That was rude and ungrateful."

"I'll forgive you if you'll join me for dinner."

I try to think of a reasonable excuse not to, but everything I come up with sounds like I'm assuming he has suspicious intentions. So I say, "Okay."

"All right, then. I'll swing by your room in twenty minutes?"

"See you then."

I click off the phone and get out of the tub, reaching for a large white towel from the nearby rack. Do I feel guilty? Should I?

It's just dinner, and it would be rude to make Jacob eat by himself. That's all it is, and since I know this, that's all that matters.

The doorbell rings. I shrug into a thick white robe and walk to the door.

The bellman on the other side gives me a wide white smile and says, "Good evening. I believe these are for you." He hands me two bags with the hotel logo on the sides.

"Thank you," I say.

"You are welcome. Enjoy your evening."

I close the door and peer inside the bags, pulling out a tissue-paper wrapped dress. I remove the paper and lift it out, instantly loving it. It's my favorite color of blue, like the ocean just beyond my room. The fabric is soft and obviously expensive. The other bag holds a pair of strappy heels that go perfectly with the dress.

I step out of the robe and slip it on. It fits perfectly, and I realize I hadn't expected it to.

I slide on the shoes and then step in front of the bathroom

dressing mirror. I look as if I'm going out to dinner with someone I seriously care about impressing. And I instantly feel guilty again.

I should stay in the room, tell Jacob I don't feel right about this. But there's a knock at the door, and he's calling out, "Ready?"

"You said twenty minutes," I call back.

"I decided that would give you too much time to change your mind. So here I am."

I stare at my reflection in the mirror, see the indecision on my face. But I can't tell him I'm not going now. I'm dressed. He's here. Quick dinner. Then bed. Alone.

♪

Holden

"I FEEL LIKE a third wheel," I say, looking at Thomas and Lila sitting across the table from me.

"And I feel like I won the lottery," Lila says, smiling at me. "Two gorgeous country music stars all to myself."

Thomas leans over and kisses the side of her neck. "I say we're the lucky ones."

"Why don't I leave you two to a romantic dinner?" I ask.

Lila reaches across the table and puts her hand on mine. "Because we want you here."

"And," Thomas says, "we wanted to see what you think of the place. We're investors."

I lean back a little and give Thomas a look. "My boy is all grown up."

Thomas laughs. "Aren't you supposed to diversify?"

"You are," I agree, looking around the place. "It's definitely happening."

The restaurant is located downtown, the decor a hip wood and leather with huge framed mirrors on every wall. It feels like a place that will get popular fast.

Just then, two tall twenty-something blondes walk over to our table. They're both wearing black and look like they could be models.

"You're Holden and Thomas," the one on the left says, looking at me.

"We are," I say.

"We really love your music," the other one says. "I'm Paige, and this is Greta."

"Nice to meet you, Paige and Greta," Thomas says. "Y'all having fun tonight?"

"We are. Even more now that we've met you two."

19

"Female at the table," Lila says, waving a hand in their direction.

They both look at her and start apologizing. "We're sorry," Paige says. "We've never been star-struck before, I guess."

"That's all right," Lila says, smiling at them. "I've kind of been there."

"You're Lila," Greta says.

"My better half," Thomas says, putting his hand around Lila's shoulders.

"I can see that," Paige says, and then looking at me, "You're without yours though?"

"Yeah," I say, feeling the stab of that all over again.

Paige looks as if she's sorry she mentioned it. "Well, we didn't mean to interrupt your dinner. Just wanted to say keep up the great music. Y'all have a great night."

They walk away from the table and over to the bar where a few guys look glad to see them.

"CeCe better get back quick," Lila says. "Isn't she coming in tomorrow?"

"She was supposed to. Looks like they might be staying a few days," I say.

Thomas and Lila both look as if they have no idea what to say.

"Why?" Thomas finally asks.

"The baby they were bringing back is sick."

"That's terrible," Lila says.

"Yeah," I say. "It is."

"Do they think she'll be all right?"

"I don't know any more than that."

"Have you talked to her?" Thomas asks.

I shake my head.

"You should call her, Holden," Lila says softly. "A lot can get read between the lines when you're just texting."

"She's right, man," Thomas says. "Go call her."

"Maybe later," I say, putting it off because I don't trust myself to say the right thing when we do finally talk. "Let's just enjoy the meal, okay?"

Thomas clearly wants to argue but makes an obvious attempt to do as I asked when the waiter shows up to take our orders. And I'm grateful for the change of subject.

♪

CeCe

THE RESTAURANT SITS directly over the water. Lights shine down from the edges of the roof, making the water transparent so that we can see the colorful fish swimming below.

"This is incredible, Jacob," I say.

He looks up from his menu, looking pleased that I like it. "It's my favorite restaurant anywhere. I'm glad I'm getting to show it to you."

I open my menu, trying not to notice how sincere he is in admitting that. "What do you recommend?"

"Everything is fresh. All the vegetables are grown locally. They have an amazing vegetable plate with whatever they picked earlier in the day."

"Sounds good."

"How long have you been vegetarian?"

"Since I watched *Food, Inc.* when I was in high school. Our health teacher showed the documentary in class one day. I had no idea. It was horrifying."

"What do you mean?"

"Seeing exactly what happens to animals that are raised for slaughter. I could never be a part of that again."

"Should I watch it?"

"I think everyone should watch it," I say. "It's good to know what we're endorsing."

"I have to admit that driving down the Interstate and seeing those tractor trailers loaded with cows makes me feel kind of sick."

"I can never let myself look. One time I did and saw the terror in one of the cow's eyes. I've dreamed about that look so many times. I don't want any part in being responsible for that kind of suffering."

Jacob closes his menu abruptly. "I think I'll have the veggie plate tonight."

"You don't have to do that for me."

He looks straight at me, his eyes sincere. "I'd do pretty much anything for you, CeCe."

Instantly, I realize I've taken this in a dangerous direction. "Jacob—"

He raises a hand, smiling at me. "I know. Don't go there. Stop sign fully noted."

He picks up his menu and opens it. "Which salad do you think looks good?"

♪

Holden

WE'RE DEBATING DESSERT when Lila's phone rings.

"Babysitter," she says and picks it up, placing a hand over her ear so that she can hear above the noise in the restaurant. She listens for several moments and then says, "We'll leave now."

"What's wrong, babe?" Thomas asks as she clicks off the call.

"She said Lexie's not feeling well. Upset tummy, she thinks. We should probably go."

"You two go on," I say. "I've got the check."

"But we invited you," Lila says.

"Go. I've got it."

Thomas slides out of the booth seat. "Thanks, man. Next one's on us. Sorry for the early depart."

"No problem. Let me know how she is."

"We will," Lila says.

Thomas hands Lila her purse and then looks at me. "Now don't you sit here and drown your sorrows until you're not safe to drive home."

"Don't worry about me," I say, "all grown up here."

"Yeah, but remember, I know you," he says.

"Y'all get out of here," I say. "I'm good."

Thomas raises a hand as they leave, and it's clear he's not sure he agrees with me.

I signal the waitress for the check. She brings it over with a smile and then leaves with my credit card. I pull my phone out of my pocket, glance to see if there's a new text from CeCe, but there's not, so I put it back, even as I realize I should be the one texting her.

"Did you get left all alone?"

Paige is standing beside the booth, looking at me with a sympathetic smile.

"They had to get home," I say.

"Does that mean you have to?" she asks.

The obvious answer is yes. But my pride has pushed its way back to front and center, and I find myself saying, "Nope. What'd you have in mind?"

"A drink at the bar would be a nice start," she says.

The waitress returns with my credit card. I sign the check, add the tip and look up at Paige, "Right behind you."

♪

CeCe

AT SOME POINT, I realize I've left my phone in the room, but somehow I manage to put the fact that I've yet to talk to Holden at the back of my mind and just enjoy the dinner.

Jacob is right about the food. It's incredible. Burrata cheese with tomatoes and arugula to start. A chick pea pasta with pine nuts and olive oil as my main dish. I'm too full for dessert when the waiter comes back with the menus. I ask for coffee instead.

"Good choices," Jacob says. "I very much liked my first vegetarian meal."

"Jacob," I say, giving him a direct look. "You need to find yourself a single girl."

"What?" he asks. "I thought we were talking about food."

"You could have pretty much anyone you want," I say, ignoring his protest.

"Obviously, I can't."

I tilt my head, letting him see my exasperation. "A psychiatrist could have a field day with you."

He puts a hand to his chest, feigning hurt, and then laughing a little when he says, "Now you know you have to explain that."

The waiter returns with my coffee, along with the after-dinner drink Jacob had ordered. I wait until he leaves the table before saying, "You pick women you won't really have to commit to."

"What if I said I like being in a relationship?"

"A real relationship is hard work."

"If it's real love, should it be hard?"

"Love isn't hard, but commitment is."

"Define commitment."

"Putting the person you love before yourself."

"Is that what you did for Holden by agreeing to come on this trip?" The question is dead serious, and if I had any illusions about Jacob not knowing exactly what he's doing, I don't now.

I answer him truthfully. "No. It isn't. And we're both suffering for it."

"Does loving someone mean you can't ever be something apart from them?"

I take a sip of my coffee, delaying the answer. When I put the cup back down, I say, "I don't think it means that, no. But it does mean you have to keep trying to grow in the same direction."

"And be careful of the forks in the road?"

"Yes," I say.

"Is that where you are now?" he asks, again dead direct.

"No," I deny. "I'm here because I wanted to help, even if you did force my hand at first. And I don't know, maybe I needed to lose myself in something different for a little while."

Jacob reaches across the table and covers my hand with his. "I'm sorry. I'm a complete jerk."

"At least we're being honest with each other," I say, moving my hand to my lap.

He sits back in his chair, glances out at the water beyond our table. When he looks at me again, his expression is thoughtful. "I'm not usually very good at that part."

"Being honest?"

"Not in relationships."

"Why?"

He shrugs, twirls the port in his glass and says, "For the most part, I've found that people use love against you."

"What does that mean?"

"You have to admit it can be a pretty handy weapon."

"If you're with someone who is willing to use it that way, they're not the right someone."

"And I've been good at picking that kind of someone."

I hear pain in his voice, and I have to believe it's real. "You put up a good front, Jacob. But underneath what you show the world, I think there's a man who wants to give a good girl his best."

"I would give you that, CeCe," he says, his eyes intent on mine.

I push my coffee cup away, saying, "We should get some sleep. Sounds like a long day tomorrow."

He wants to argue, makes no move to hide it. But he doesn't, signing the check the waiter had left on the table, then standing up and saying, "Sleep it is."

♪

Holden

SECOND DRINK AND I've already conceded to not driving myself home. A taxi will do, and I have to admit, it feels good to let go a little bit and stop thinking about everything that feels so wrong right now.

Paige and Greta have started a game of quarters on the bar. I neglect to tell them about the frat championship I won in college. But Greta seems to be enjoying losing a little too much, and slips off the bar stool, nearly hitting the floor before I catch her with my right arm.

"My hero," she says, tucking herself up against me and nuzzling my neck with a drunken giggle.

"Whoa there, SuperWoman," Paige says, pulling her friend off me and adding, "Married man here, remember?"

"Oh, like you care about that," Greta says with another giggle. "All he'd have to do is say the word and you'd be out the door with him so fast my head would spin. I mean your head would spin."

Paige smiles at this, gives me a look of apology and says, "I'd better get her home."

"Are you okay to drive?" I ask.

"Guilty as accused," she says. "Hey, I can give you a ride too if you don't want to drive."

"I'll get a cab."

"I'm a good driver," she says. "A taxi's no fun."

I know better. The little voice inside me says, "Get the cab, Holden." I have no explanation then for why I find myself saying, "Okay. Thanks. I'll take you up on it."

♪

Holden

GRETA'S PLACE IS the first stop because she doesn't live far from the restaurant. She's still giggling from the back seat when Paige pulls into the parking lot of the apartment complex.

"Girl, you need to go sleep this off," Paige says, turning around to look at her.

"Never going to believe what I just did," Greta says.

I also turn to look at her then, spotting my phone in her hand.

"What did you do, Gret?" Paige asks, grabbing the phone.

"Just made a little video of you and Holden," she says, slurring the end of my name, "and sent it to his wife."

"You what?" Paige asks, her anger with her friend suddenly clear. She hands me the phone, and I check the texts to see that she has indeed sent a video to CeCe. I lean my head back against the seat and blow out a sigh.

"Holden, I'm so sorry. I had no idea she had your phone."

"Yeah, me either," I say.

"Let me get her inside her apartment, and I'll drive you home."

I'd like to say I'll walk, but since it's better than ten miles away, I say, "I'll carry her up. I'm not sure she'll make it on foot."

I get out, open the back door and lean in to lift Greta out of the seat. All of a sudden she's not looking like she's feeling too well, and I'm hoping she makes it upstairs.

"You're such a gentleman," she says, her cheek pressed against my shirt. "I'm sorry for sending that video. I probably got you in a whole lot of trouble. And you're such a nice guy too."

"Greta, I think you're better off not saying anymore," Paige says, sticking a key in the lock of the apartment door.

She steps inside the foyer and waves me down a short hallway to Greta's bedroom. I lower her onto the bed. She's already falling asleep.

"Should we wait here to make sure she's okay?" I ask.

"You've taken enough abuse for one evening," Paige says. "I'll come back by after I drop you off."

"Are you sure?"

"Yes," she says. "She'll be fine."

A few minutes later, we're back in the car, silence hanging between us. I give her my address. She keys it into her GPS.

"I'm so sorry for all of this," Paige says, glancing at me with genuine apology in her eyes. "I still can't believe she—"

"Don't worry about it," I say. "It's not your fault."

"If it would help, I'll be glad to call your wife and tell her you didn't do anything."

I glance out the window, shaking my head. "No need. I'm not sure she'll care anyway."

"Oh." She hesitates, and then, "Rough patch?"

"Sort of."

"Everybody goes through those. From what I've seen about you and CeCe in the press, y'all have that once-in-a-lifetime-kind-of-thing."

"Even those hit rough patches," I say.

"I wouldn't know," she says. "I haven't found that yet."

I look over at her. "How old are you?"

"Twenty-two."

"Be patient. He'll come along."

"I'm starting to wonder."

"You're a nice girl, Paige. Don't settle for anything other than that."

"When you first met CeCe, did you know she was the one?"

"I was actually in another relationship at the time. And I thought she was the one. But when I met CeCe, I suddenly understood that I had no idea what that was."

"That's so romantic," Paige says.

"It was also really hard."

"How so?"

"Sarah, the other girl in my life, we'd been together a long time. I didn't want to hurt her. She had been really sick, and I wanted to be there for her."

"Is she okay?" Paige asks, concerned.

"She is. Actually, she found a great guy, and she's really happy."

"If you'd had a crystal ball, you could have saved yourself a lot of agony."

"Yeah, it all worked out in the end. But you're right. You don't know that when you're in the middle of it, trying to figure things out."

Paige takes the exit off the highway, and we drive in silence for a stretch before I say, "No boyfriend in the picture?"

"Nope, free as a bird right now," she says, shrugging.

"So what brings you to Nashville?"

"The usual suspects."

"Writing or singing or both?"

"Both," she says, smiling at me.

"Made any headway?"

"A bit. Have to admit it's a daunting process."

"The trick is not to put any stop clocks on it."

"What do you mean?"

"A lot of people come to town thinking it's all going to happen overnight, and in 99 percent of our cases, it doesn't. Once I decided to focus on writing the best songs I could write instead of beating myself up about the fact that I didn't have any on the radio yet, that's when the whole thing started to make sense."

"A girl's gotta eat though," she says.

"True. That's what second jobs are for. Do what it takes to pay the bills, and leave a chunk of your day for working on your art."

"Is that what you did?"

"Yeah. Bartending paid mine."

"Waitressing," she says.

"That's what CeCe did," I say, letting myself remember those times at the restaurant and how much fun we had.

"I remember reading that somewhere," Paige says.

"They were good days," I say. "We were all hot to climb the ladder, but looking back, those were great times."

"Is it not what you thought it would be?"

I don't answer for a couple of seconds, deciding not to give her a pat answer. "Maybe it's like most things," I say. "It's never exactly what you imagined it would be."

"See from where I'm sitting, you're on top of the world," she says.

"I don't mean to sound unappreciative. I know how lucky I am. But maybe the point is to also enjoy the journey along the way. Because that part is better than you think it is."

It's almost two a.m., and the street is completely empty of cars. Paige slows at our driveway and turns in.

"Wow," she says. "What an incredible place."

I hit the code on my phone, and the gate swings open.

Just in front of the house, she stops the car and says, "I can't tell you how much I enjoyed meeting you tonight, Holden. Your CeCe is one lucky girl."

"You too, Paige. Thanks for the ride."

"If you get in too much trouble over that video, let me know, and I'll set her straight."

"I think this is my hole to dig out of," I admit, opening the car door and sliding out. Leaning in, I say, "Hey, drop off a demo if you'd like. I'll take a listen and see if I can direct it somewhere for you."

"Really?" she asks, smiling her surprise.

"Sure," I say. "Be happy to."

"Thank you so much. You're awesome, Holden Ashford."

♪

CeCe

JACOB WALKS ME to my room, and if I had expected him to try something, I was wrong. He's the perfect gentleman.

"I'll get a wake-up call for seven," he says. "Sound good?"

"Sure," I say, even though I'm certain I'll be awake long before then because I never sleep as well away from home.

"Good night, CeCe," he says, turning to walk back down the hall.

Inside the room, housekeeping has left the lamps on by the bed, a bottle of water, and two pieces of chocolate on the nightstand. My phone is on the desk where I'd left it. I pick it up and swipe the screen for messages.

I feel instant relief at the sight of Holden's name. I sit down on the side of the bed, open the text, but there are no words, just a video.

I tap play, and at first the screen is dark. It's inside a car, I think, and the radio is playing. I hear a girl giggling, and then the focus clears. Holden is in the passenger seat of a car, and a girl I've never seen before is driving. They're talking. I make out a few words, but it's mostly muffled.

The camera drops, and there's a lot of noise like the person filming is trying to pick it up. And then the screen goes black.

I sit for a moment, too numb to know what to think. I hit play again, watch it through one more time. I feel like the room has been turned upside down, and I'm trying to find my way back to vertical.

Somehow, I know he didn't mean for this to be sent to me. Does he know it was? Should I call him?

My fingers type the text before I give myself time to think about it.

Guess you're not lonely after all.

I turn the phone off then and toss it on the desk, suddenly wanting nothing more than sleep and its immediate escape.

♪

Holden

I'VE JUST COME back in the house from letting Hank Junior and Patsy out when I hear my phone ding on the kitchen counter.

I pick it up, read the message from CeCe and hit the call button. Her voice mail instantly picks up. "Hey," I say. "Call me back, will you?"

I look up to find Hank sitting a few feet away, studying me with a worried expression. "It's all right, boy. Everything's okay."

But as soon as I say the words, I realize I have no idea whether they're true or not.

♪

CeCe

I SPEND A RESTLESS night, trying to sleep instead of thinking about the video or what it might mean. I'm awake though more than asleep, and when I meet Jacob downstairs at eight o'clock for coffee, he looks rested and fresh while I look the opposite.

"Everything okay?" he asks, taking a sip from his cup. "You look tired."

"I'm fine," I say. "Just didn't sleep great."

He doesn't ask why even though I suspect he's guessing there's a reason.

We're back at the orphanage by nine. A van is sitting in the parking lot when we arrive, a couple of ladders sticking out of the back.

An older man with white hair and an even whiter smile greets us with, "So we have some work to do again?"

"Sure do," Jacob says, reaching out to shake his hand. "Thanks for coming on short notice."

"More than happy to," he says, his gaze falling to me.

"This is my friend, CeCe Ashford," Jacob says, introducing us.

The man sticks out his hand and says, "I'm Alexandro. Only Jacob could bring such beauty to our country."

"Last time I was here," Jacob says, "Alexandro gave me some lessons on how to flirt. You see why I signed up, CeCe?"

I smile and shake my head. "I don't think either one of you needs lessons."

Alexandro laughs good-naturedly. "Ah, so Jacob has been practicing on you?"

Mrs. Castellanos comes out of the building just then, asking Jacob if she can speak to us for a moment. He tells Alexandro we'll be right back, and we follow her to her office.

She closes the door behind us and says, "I just received a call from the doctor about Giovanna. I'm afraid she does have pneumonia in her right lung. They are treating her with intravenous antibiotics."

"What is her prognosis?" Jacob asks, concern underscoring the words.

"They describe it as a mild case. If you both would like to visit her in the hospital this afternoon, I am happy to take you there."

Jacob glances at me, and I nod. "Yes," he says. "We'd like that."

"We'll leave around three?" she says.

"Sure. Until then, we'll get busy."

"Thank you both so very much. I can't tell you how grateful I am for what you're doing. Both for Giovanna and for the work on the building today. To be honest, there are days when I'm not sure how it will all work out, but then God sends an answer through someone like you, and I wonder why I worried."

Her words are heartfelt and touching. I am newly glad to be here and be a part of it.

We're on the way back to meet the painter when Jacob stops me with a hand on my arm. "Look, CeCe, I know you didn't sign on for this. It was supposed to be a quick trip here and back. I don't know how long it will end up taking, but if you don't want to stay, I understand. I can get you a flight back. It's not a problem."

Logically, I know this would make sense. Holden and I are a mess. I need to get home and try to fix what we've broken. But I'm already shaking my head because something inside me needs to see this through. "I'm staying," I say.

And without another word, we walk on.

♪

Holden

THOMAS AND I meet at our favorite coffee shop on Broadway just before ten o'clock. We were supposed to meet at the studio, but I asked him to come here first. We've gotten our coffee and sat down at a table in the back when he says, "What's up? You look like hell."

I take a sip of the hot coffee, and then say in a low voice, "CeCe isn't answering my calls."

"Is she all right?" Thomas asks, instantly concerned.

"I don't know." I set the coffee down, push the cup away. "After you and Lila left the restaurant last night, I hung out for a while with those two girls, Paige and Greta."

"Yeah?" Thomas says, his tone indicating he knows what's coming.

"It wasn't like that. We just played some quarters. Greta got a little drunk. Paige drove her home and offered to take me too. Somewhere along the way, Greta managed to get my phone and send a video of Paige and me to CeCe."

"What?" Thomas makes five syllables of the question.

"We weren't doing anything except driving, but I guess it didn't look good."

"You think?"

"I know. It was stupid to put myself in that position."

"Have you talked to CeCe?"

I shake my head. "She sent a text."

"She's pissed."

"You could say."

"How long before they come back?"

"No idea."

"Then you better get yourself to Belize, brother."

"I can't just show up there out of the blue."

39

"Do I need to remind you that your wife is out of the country with Jacob Bartley? And now you've given her serious reason to pay you back?"

Put like that, I feel an instant need to jump on the next plane. "Hopefully, she'll answer her phone this morning."

Thomas gives me a long look. "I wouldn't be waiting around for it. If I were you, I'd be on my way to Belize."

♪

CeCe

JACOB ACTUALLY HAS a really good sense of humor and the admirable quality of directing it at himself instead of others.

He puts it to work with me and the group of guys helping us paint the orphanage's main playroom. At one point, he demonstrates what his singing sounded like before his voice changed, and one of the painters laughs so hard, I'm amazed he doesn't fall off his ladder.

When the men break for lunch, I use the sink in the corner of the room to get the paint off my hands, looking at Jacob and saying, "I think you missed your calling."

"What?" he asks, grinning.

"You could have been Leno."

"I learned early on it's far better to get them laughing with you instead of at you."

"Yeah, but not everyone has the gift."

"Can I be honest for a sec?"

"Sure."

"You don't look as if you feel too much like laughing."

I shrug, trying not to dissolve into tears, which is exactly what I'm about to do. "Just tired, I guess."

He walks over, puts a hand on my shoulder. "Hey, what is it? Talk to me."

"It's nothing—"

"Nothing doesn't make you cry."

"I'm not crying." But I stop there, because all of a sudden, I am crying, a ridiculous gush of tears that I cannot for the life of me stop.

"Hey. Come here," Jacob says, reaching out to pull me into his arms. I absolutely know this is not a place I should be, that I should pull away. Now. Immediately. But I can't deny needing the comfort, and so I don't make myself.

"What happened?" he asks softly.

My face is against his shirt, my voice muffled when I say, "It's stupid."

"If it makes you cry, it's not stupid."

I don't say anything for several moments, but he just waits, rubbing a hand across the back of my hair.

"I got a video on my phone last night of Holden out with some girl."

Jacob pulls back, looks down at me, surprised. "Who sent it?"

I shake my head. "It came from Holden's phone."

"He sent it?"

"I don't know."

"You know I have my bias, but gotta say that doesn't sound like Holden."

I can't deny it. It doesn't. Nonetheless, I watched it with my own eyes.

"There's probably a very reasonable explanation," Jacob says. "You know by now that fans can pull some crazy stuff."

I look up at him, studying his face for a moment. "I thought you'd be the first one to suggest hanging him."

"I believe in fighting fair," he says, shrugging.

"You're not as simple as you make yourself out to be, are you?"

"Complicated is way more interesting, don't you think?"

I laugh a little, stepping away from him and saying, "Actually, I think I'm the one not playing fair."

"What do you mean?"

"I shouldn't be turning to you for comfort, Jacob."

"Do you hear me complaining?"

"No. Thanks. For listening."

"Anytime."

His gaze hooks with mine, lingering for several long seconds before he claps his hands together and says, "I'm starved. I asked the hotel to put together a cooler of sandwiches for us. Ready to eat?"

I start to tell him I'm not hungry, but since he was thoughtful enough to go to all the trouble, I say, "Sure. That sounds great."

♪

CeCe

LATER THAT AFTERNOON, Mrs. Castellanos rides in the van with us to the hospital.

She points out interesting things along the way, but I mostly listen, still thinking about Holden and the text I sent him earlier asking if we can talk later tonight. His response had been a brief **sure, what time?**

I texted back **ten o'clock**, wanting to be certain I was in the hotel room before calling. My stomach drops at the thought of it, and I wonder how so much emotional distance could have developed between us in such a short time.

"Here we are," Mrs. Castellanos says as the van slows for a turn into the parking lot of an enormous, modern-looking building.

The driver lets us off at the front entrance, telling Jacob he will wait for us in one of the nearby visitor spaces.

The hospital is surprisingly up to date. I'm not sure why I had expected otherwise, but it looks like most of the hospitals I have seen in the United States.

The pediatric unit is on the fourth floor. We take the elevator in silence, following Mrs. Castellanos to the nurse's desk. She speaks with a smiling woman there who directs us to follow her down a hallway to a room with a long glass window where we can see a dozen babies in neonatal cribs.

"There she is," Mrs. Castellanos says, pointing at a tiny baby on the second row back from us. "Our Giovanna."

I stare at the little girl's face, her eyes shut, her pink lips making a sucking motion, as if she is hungry. Her dark hair is surprisingly thick, and her tiny feet kick the air. She's quiet though, and I realize that it seems as if she should be crying, voicing her desire for food or to be held.

"She's beautiful," I say, completely captured by this tiny angel.

44

"She is," Jacob agrees.

"I'm biased, of course, but she has stolen our hearts," Mrs. Castellanos says.

"Is it possible for us to hold her?" I ask, expecting the answer to be no.

"Let's ask the nurse," Mrs. Castellanos says. She waves at one of the women in white dresses behind the glass. The woman comes to the door and listens while Mrs. Castellanos asks her something in spanish. The nurse nods, smiles, and beckons us inside the room.

We stand by Giovanna's crib, while the nurse reaches down to pick her up, adjusting the lines attached to her so that they do not pull.

"Who would like to hold her first?" she asks, looking at Jacob and then at me.

"CeCe, you go ahead. I'm not very experienced with holding babies."

I immediately put out my arms for her, my heart pounding hard.

She is so light that it's like holding feathers. I look into her sweet face, and she opens her eyes, staring up at me with such brilliant innocence that I am hit with a wave of feeling, so intense it sucks the breath from my lungs.

The nurse indicates I should sit in the chair behind me. I lower myself carefully onto the seat, afraid of dropping her, of hurting her. And all I know is I am hopelessly, irreversibly, in love.

♪

CeCe

AT MY INSISTENCE, Jacob takes a turn holding Giovanna. He's actually a lot better at it than he'd indicated he would be. He holds his finger out, and she latches tightly onto it, bringing an instant smile to Jacob's face.

Mrs. Castellanos had stepped out to speak to a doctor, and she returns now with a look of relief on her face. "Good news," she says. "They are feeling much better about the pneumonia. Her lungs are already more clear than they were even yesterday."

"That's wonderful," I say. "When will she be able to leave the hospital?"

"He says we should know something by tomorrow."

"Would you like to hold her once more before we go?" Jacob asks me.

I very much do, and I take her gently from his arms, holding her tiny body against my chest and feeling suddenly forlorn at the thought of leaving her here alone.

A nurse appears with a bottle, saying, "Time for dinner."

I hand Giovanna to her, swamped with an instant, tangible sadness.

"I will check on her in the morning," Mrs. Castellanos tells the nurse as we leave the room.

Just before we reach the parking lot, Mrs. Castellanos says, "I've asked my husband to pick me up. He'll be here in a few minutes. Thank you for coming with me to see her."

"It was our pleasure," Jacob tells her. "See you tomorrow."

We wave goodbye, and it's only after we're back in the van that

Jacob puts his hand over mine and says, "That was hard for you, wasn't it?"

I stare out the window as we leave the parking lot, not meeting his gaze when I say, "I haven't let myself think too much about the baby we lost. I really haven't been able to. But holding her, Giovanna, made it all so real."

"I'm really sorry that happened to you," Jacob says in a low voice, "and to Holden."

"Me too," I say. "I think I'm only now truly realizing what a loss it was."

We don't say anything for a good while as the van leaves the city behind and heads for the charter boat that will get us back to our hotel.

"It's hard to believe she doesn't have anyone," I say, looking at him.

"It is," he agrees. "And she has a hard road ahead of her."

"It doesn't seem fair, does it?"

"No. But that's why we're here. To help her."

"I'm so glad that we came."

"Are you?" he asks, meeting my gaze. "It's been way more than I originally asked of you."

"And I've already gotten way more from it than I ever imagined I would."

"Really?"

I nod. "Really. So thank you. For asking me to come."

"You know what, CeCe Ashford?"

"What?"

"I really like you."

Something in his voice makes me realize that he's not flirting. That this isn't about anything other than him liking who I am as a human being. And I have to say that feels kind of nice.

♪

Holden

THEY SAY MISERY loves company, but I wouldn't want to inflict mine on anyone else.

Our time in the studio had been pretty much a waste as far as my contribution was concerned. Thomas had finally taken pity on me, or maybe himself, and suggested we call it a day.

So now I'm at home, alone, wondering if I should do exactly what Thomas thought I should do and hop on a plane to Belize.

In the kitchen, I sit down in front of my laptop and pull up Expedia. I do a search for flights out of Nashville and wait for the options to come up.

There are several, and I stare at them, trying to decide what's right.

I could go. Surprise her.

But as soon as the thought comes to me, I'm thinking what if she sees it as me not trusting her.

Do I?

Yes.

Do I trust Jacob?

No.

Even so, I can't see myself just showing up in Belize. If CeCe wants me there, I'll go. And the only way to know the answer to that is to ask her.

♪

CeCe

I WISH I could call Holden now. Clear the air between us. Talk about the stupid video and then forget it.

I have so much I want to tell him about Giovanna, how it had felt to hold her. How precious she is. We're only a few miles from the boat dock, but I suddenly can't wait to get there, to get to my room where I can call him alone.

I hear something coming up behind the van and turn to see two motorcycles, or dirt bikes, racing up so close I'm sure they're going to hit us. "Jacob," I say. "What are they doing?"

He looks at the driver and says, "What's going on?"

The driver hits the accelerator, and the van lurches forward. There's a curve just ahead, and as we head into it, it feels as if the van is tipping up on the left side. I grab the sides of my seat, clutching as hard as I can, my heart suddenly pounding in my ears.

"What's going on?" Jacob says again to the driver, this time raising his voice.

"I am not sure," the driver says. "But it is best to get you to the dock."

Jacob puts his hand over mine. "It's okay. We're almost there."

The road has straightened out now. Both motorcycles cut around the van, flying past us on the left. A car is coming toward us in the other lane, blowing its horn and blinking its lights. Both motorcycles cut back over in front of us just in time to miss a head-on collision with the car.

"What are they doing, Jacob?" I ask, hearing the fear in my voice.

"Just being jerks," he says, and I can tell he's trying not to let me hear his concern.

The bikes race a short distance ahead, and I'm thinking it's over when they suddenly slam on the brakes and do a U-turn in the middle of the road. Our driver has to stop or run over them. A couple of seconds pass during which he does not hit the brake, and I'm afraid that's exactly what he's going to do.

"Stop!" Jacob says, and the driver slams the brake to the floor.

We come to a tire-squealing stop right in front of the bikes. The engine stalls.

Both of the men have on helmets with full-face visors. They're off and running toward the van before we can say a word. Jacob slides across the seat and puts his arm around my shoulders, pulling me against him in a gesture of protection.

"Get down!" the driver yells out, slamming the locks of the van.

It's only then that I see both men have guns. They're pointing them at the driver through the passenger-side window.

"Open the doors!" one of the men yells.

The driver tries to start the van. It makes a sluggish noise and then turns over.

The man points the gun at the driver and suddenly the window shatters. The driver slumps forward against the steering wheel, blood gushing from the side of his head.

I scream, the sound reverberating through the van. Jacob unsnaps his seat belt and throws himself in front of me.

"Get down, CeCe!" he yells.

One of the men reaches through the broken window and releases the lock, yanking open the door.

"Get out!" he shouts at us.

"You'll have to shoot me first," Jacob says.

"That can be arranged," the man says, pointing the gun directly at Jacob's chest.

"No!" I scream. "Jacob, do what he says!"

"CeCe, we can't," he says, pushing me back behind him.

Just then, another car races up behind the van, cutting over to our right on the shoulder of the road and skidding to a stop.

"In the car!" the man yells at us. "Or we'll shoot you both. Your choice."

I am shaking so hard I can't get air into my lungs. "We have to do what he says, Jacob," I say, glancing at the driver slumped across the steering wheel. It's clear that he's dead. I start to cry. "They're going to kill us if we don't."

"What do you want?" Jacob yells at the men.

"For you to do as we say now," the man screams back, still pointing the gun directly at Jacob.

"Okay," I say, sliding past Jacob and taking his hand to pull him forward. I can't stand the thought of waiting to see whether they're serious and one or both of us end up dead.

Jacob locks his fingers with mine, attempting to keep me half-behind him as we slide out of the van. One of the men opens the back door of the car and shoves us inside.

There's a panel between the back seat and the front, and we can't see the driver. The doors lock with a thunk, and the car peels onto the asphalt. I glance back to see the men jump onto the motorcycles and take off after us.

"Why are they doing this, Jacob?" I say, my voice trembling.

He shakes his head, and there's fear on his face when he says, "I think we're being kidnapped."

♪

Holden

IT'S ELEVEN O'CLOCK, and I still haven't heard from CeCe.

She said she would call me at ten. I waited with my phone right beside me, and then I started calling her, but there was no answer, each call clicking straight to voice mail.

Is she so mad at me that she's decided she doesn't want to talk? I guess it's a possibility, but CeCe isn't one for games, so somehow, that doesn't sit right with me.

Midnight. No answer to my texts or calls. A direct call to her hotel room with no answer now has me worried.

I pace the kitchen floor, Hank Junior awake and watching me with a concerned expression.

"What should I do?" I ask, looking down at him.

Hank whines, gets up, and circles the room once before walking back over to sit next to me. I think he would tell me if he could.

I don't want to do it, but I can't sleep until I know she's okay. I walk to the refrigerator and look at the note CeCe had left with Jacob's cell number written on it.

I wait then while the phone rings and rings. His voice comes on – *leave a message* – and that's it.

"Damn it!" Frustrated, I slam my phone on the kitchen counter. My wife is in another country, out of touch, and I have no way of knowing whether she's okay or not.

Hank follows me upstairs, his footsteps behind me sounding as dejected as I feel.

♪

CeCe

WITH GUNS POINTED at our backs, the two men shove us inside a small, concrete building, pulling the door closed behind us and snapping a lock shut on the outside. They had taken our phones, searching us both to make sure we had nothing else on us.

There are no windows in the building, and only a small lamp in a far corner of the room. A narrow door leads to a bathroom with a dirty-looking toilet and sink, but again, no window.

Jacob and I stare at each other, silent, as if we are both in shock.

"They'll make some kind of demand," he says, his voice not quite as certain as I would hope for it to be. "We're going to be fine."

"Why us?" I ask. "And how did they know who we were? That we would be in the van?"

Jacob shakes his head, and I can see the same shock I'm feeling reflected in his face.

He paces back and forth in the dim light of the room, raking a hand through his hair. "Let's just think for a minute. There has to be a way out of here."

We both start to look then, examining in minute detail every speck of space. Walls: concrete block. Doors: all three made of heavy metal and locked.

I slide to the floor, pulling my knees to my chest and lowering my head to stare at the floor. Jacob sits down next to me, leaning against the wall behind us.

"Shit," he says.

"Do you think they're going to kill us?" I ask. I honestly can't believe I'm saying this out loud, but truthfully, I'm surprised they haven't already.

"No," he says quickly. "We're not worth anything if we're dead."

The words shock me, and I look over at him, saying, "You really think that's what this is? That we've been kidnapped?"

"I don't know what else it could be. Otherwise, they would have just shot us along with the driver."

"Oh," I say, thinking again of the driver and the awful way in which his life had been ended. I start to cry again, and Jacob puts his arm around my shoulder, pulling me close.

"Shh," he says. "Don't think about it. Not now. We know he didn't suffer."

"This is insane," I say. And then I think about Holden. "I was supposed to call Holden tonight. He has to be wondering why I haven't."

"Do you think he'll call the hotel?"

"Probably, but nobody there will be able to tell him anything," I say.

"If he doesn't get an answer fairly quickly, I think he'll get persistent. If you were my wife, I would."

Ordinarily, I would agree with him. Holden is very protective of me. But this time might be different.

"What?" Jacob asks, when I drop my head against the wall.

"We were kind of having a thing."

"A thing?"

"A fight, I guess."

"About you being here?"

I shake my head. "The video."

"So he might think you're just not answering your phone because you don't want to talk to him?"

"Maybe," I say, miserable.

"That sucks."

"Yeah. Will anyone miss you?"

"Sadly, no. I spoke to my manager earlier today and told him not to expect me back for a few days."

I start to cry for real now. I can't help it. The thought of dying in this place, of never seeing Holden again, Mama, Hank Junior, Patsy. And then, another thought hits me. "Giovanna."

"What?" Jacob asks.

"What if we're here too long? And she doesn't get the surgery in time?"

"Don't," Jacob says, pressing his hand into mine. "She will."

I don't say another word. I just close my eyes and start to pray.

♪

Holden

I START CALLING CeCe at seven the next morning.

Still no answer on her cell. No answer in her hotel room either. And Jacob isn't answering his.

A feeling of panic has crept into my chest, and no matter how hard I try to tell myself not to start imagining things, that is exactly what I'm doing.

It starts with what if she's run off with Jacob? But somehow, I know it's not that. That's not CeCe. Should anything between us ever get that bad, she would be up front with it. She's not the kind of person to do otherwise.

And then I start to think what if something has happened to them? A wreck and no one has found them yet?

I stop myself there, before I can come up with some other awful scenario. I do the only other thing I can think to do. I call Thomas.

♪

AND HE DOESN'T reassure me. The opposite, in fact.

"You know this isn't like her, man."

"I know it's not."

"There's got to be someone else you can call. Wait. What about the orphanage? Do you have the name of it?"

"Yeah," I say, walking to the office door and scanning the desktop for the two or three pieces of paper CeCe had printed out about it before she left. They're there at one corner. I flip them over and find a number at the bottom of the last page.

"I'll try there," I say. "I should have thought of that."

"Call me right back, okay?"

"Yeah," I say. "It might take a minute to get the country code and get through."

"I'll be waiting," he says, worry in his voice.

I do a quick online search for how to dial Belize and then punch the numbers into my phone.

The ring is tinny and distant. A woman answers in Spanish.

"Hello?" I say, wishing I spoke the language.

"Yes," she says, switching to English. "May I help you?"

"I hope so. I'm looking for my wife, CeCe Ashford."

"Ah, yes," she says. "Let me put you with our director. One moment."

Before I can thank her, she puts me on hold, and, not more than a few seconds later, a different voice comes across the line.

"Mr. Ashford," she says, and something in her tone puts me instantly on guard. "I'm Mrs. Castellanos, the director here at the orphanage."

"Yes. I'm trying to get in touch with my wife, but I haven't been able to reach her since last night."

"Yes," she says, the word sounding instantly heavy. "I am afraid I have some very bad news."

"What?" I ask, wondering if I've actually said the word out loud, my heart dropping like a boulder from a ten-story building.

"Your wife and Jacob. They are missing."

"What do you mean missing?" I ask, forcing each word out.

"They were on the way back to the hotel last night after our visit at the hospital with Giovanna, the baby they are here to help. The van they were riding in was hijacked. The driver was shot and killed."

I drop onto the desk chair, as if all the air has been let out of me. "Killed?"

"Yes," she says, and I hear the break in her voice. "The police are searching for CeCe and Jacob. I'm so sorry you haven't been contacted before now. We had trouble getting information about—"

"I will be on the next available flight there," I say, interrupting her because I can't waste another second. "Call me directly the moment you hear anything. Please." I give her the number, then repeat it to make sure she has written it down correctly.

"I'm so sorry, Mr. Ashford. If there's anything—"

But I've already hung up.

♪

I CALL THOMAS, to let him know what I've learned, but also to ask him to go with me. I don't have to ask. I've barely gotten the explanation out before he says, "Book me on that flight too. I'm coming with you."

I'm not even exactly sure how I manage it, but three hours later, we're on a flight to Miami that will connect to Belize City. Thomas and I share a two-seat row in first class, and I guess something in our faces must discourage the flight attendant from asking us anything other than would we like something to drink.

I stare out the window at the clouds below the plane's wing and feel more helpless than I have ever felt in my life.

♪

CeCe

I WAKE TO the sound of the metal door opening, the hinge squeaking as if it is rusty. Jacob must hear it at the same time, because he's scrambling to get to his feet, lunging across the room, and yelling, "Hey! Wait! Let's talk!"

There's the sound of something hitting the floor with a thud. In the dimness, I can't make out what it is before the door slams shut. There's a noise that sounds like an enormous lock clanking closed.

"Damn it!" Jacob yells.

"What did they throw in?" I ask, disappointment so heavy on my chest that I can't make myself get up.

He picks up whatever they threw in, saying, "It's a box."

"Of what?"

He walks back to where I'm sitting against the wall, putting it down next to me. "Guess we'll have to open it and see."

He tears the strip of tape from the center and opens the flaps. "Looks like bottles of water and some food."

I'd like to feel brave enough to refuse to drink or eat, but the truth is I'm not. "I'm so thirsty."

"Me too," he says, passing me a bottle.

We both turn up our bottles and drain them.

He reaches inside the box and pulls out cereal, a bunch of bananas and two bags of potato chips.

"Wonder how long this is supposed to last us," I say.

"We could ration, but I'm not sure I see the point in sitting here hungry."

He passes me a banana. I peel mine and eat it slowly, savoring the taste. "You can have all the potato chips if I can have the rest of the bananas."

Jacob smiles at me and says, "And what about my potassium needs?"

I giggle, which seems ridiculous under the circumstances. But maybe that's what you do when you've lost complete control over your life and your future.

"If you don't want to talk about it," he says, looking at me, "you don't have to, but the shooting in DC, did you think you were going to die that night?"

I put my banana peel on the floor, not quite meeting his gaze when I say, "I was certain of it. I watched him shoot people around me and then point the gun directly at me and pull the trigger."

"I heard a little about that night at some point, but I never wanted to ask too much just because I didn't want to make him relive it. It must have been a nightmare."

"It was. One we survived, but you don't ever really leave it behind."

"You've lived through some life-altering stuff."

"Yeah. Think I ought to be reconsidering this Nashville thing?"

"I'd say yes, except I'm not sure you can blame this one on Nashville. I think you can blame this one on me."

"Do you think they're after money?"

"What else?"

Just then, the door opens again, and a backpack flies across the room to land right in front of us. The door is immediately slammed shut.

Jacob reaches for the backpack, pulls it onto his lap and unzips it. From inside, he pulls an old-fashioned tape recorder with a Post-it on top that says, "Push play."

He does, and we listen as an unrecognizable voice fills the room.

"Follow our instructions, Mr. Bartley, and this will be over quickly. Should you choose not to follow our instructions, you will be determining your fate and also that of your lady friend."

The light in the room is dim, but I can see the blood leaving Jacob's face. I put my hand over his while the voice continues.

"Our next drop will be an untraceable cell phone on which you will call your bank and make a transfer to the account number we provide you with. We will be able to listen in on the call, so should you decide to ask for help instead of doing as we say, we will end your lives immediately. This doesn't have to go badly. Do as we ask and all will be well."

The play button pops off as the tape ends. Jacob hurls it across the room. It slams into the wall and flies into pieces.

I reach out and put my hand on his, squeezing hard. "How much could they want?"

"I don't know," he says, shaking his head.

"What if you don't have the amount they ask for? If they'll let me call Holden, I can—"

"They probably want to involve as few people as possible," he says.

"But what if you give them the money, and they kill us anyway?"

"It's not out of the realm of possibility," he says.

"Maybe you should refuse to do it. Make the condition that they have to let us go first."

"CeCe, I hate to say it, but I don't think we're in a position to make conditions."

"This is so wrong!"

Jacob slips his arm around my shoulder and pulls me close. "It's okay," he says. "We'll do what they say, and they'll let us go. Everything will be all right."

I want to say that he doesn't know that. We have absolutely no way of knowing that they will honor their word. Our only choice is to wait and see.

♪

Holden

WE CATCH THE first available taxi outside the Belize airport.

Thomas slides into the back seat, and I jump in behind him, giving the driver a piece of paper with the address of the police station written on it. "Can you take us there, please?" I ask.

"Certainly," he responds in barely accented English.

"Surely they'll know something by now," Thomas says, his voice low and worried.

I'm too scared to say that I hope he's right, so I stare out the window at the crowded street where an impossible number of cars, bicycles, and pedestrians are trying to filter through. The taxi is crawling along at a nearly unbearable pace. My chest feels completely constricted with the need to lower my window and beg them to let us through. "How long will it take to get there?" I ask the driver.

With a look of apology, he lifts his shoulders and says, "In this traffic, it's hard to say, sir."

"Is there any way to get around it?"

"I'm afraid not. It's one of the injustices of my city."

I want to tell him about the real injustice, the fact that someone here has
my wife, is holding her against her will. I can't let myself think of what else beyond that.

"She's going to be all right, man," Thomas says, as if he's just read my mind. "Faith has got to be your rope on this one. That's the only way to climb out of this pit."

"What if she's hurt, or—"

"Don't," Thomas says, looking at me with sympathy-filled eyes. "We can't go there."

"I should have come with her," I say, my voice so low I'm not sure Thomas can hear me above the rattle of the car engine.

But he instantly says, "How could you have known?"

"I let my pride dictate my common sense."

"Hey, I've been there. But it doesn't do us any good to dwell on what we could have done. Listen to me, sounding like the voice of wisdom here. Just don't beat yourself up. What matters now is what you do from here."

I stare out the window at the unfamiliar streets of Belize and try not to imagine CeCe hurt and scared. Or worse.

"Here we are," the driver says, turning into the circular drive of a tall building. "Would you like for me to wait for you?"

"Thanks," I say. "But I don't know how long this will take."

After I pay him, he hands me a card with his number and says, "Call me if you need a ride."

Thomas and I get out of the cab, carrying nothing but the backpacks we brought with us. Inside the building I ask the young woman at the front desk if we can see the commissioner of police. "I'm here to speak with him about my wife, CeCe Ashford."

Recognition flares across her face, instantly followed by sympathy. "Of course, Mr. Ashford," she says, quickly picking up her phone and speaking low into the receiver. She turns slightly away from us so that I can't make out what she is saying.

When she puts the phone back down, she meets my gaze and says, "Commissioner Salvidar asks that you come to his office. Please take the elevator just around the corner to the second floor. He will be waiting for you."

I thank her, and we all but run for the elevator. On the second floor, another young woman with long, dark hair meets us and asks us to follow her. At a large double door near the end of a long hallway, she says, "Please, go right in."

The office is enormous, bookshelves lining the wall to our right. In the center of the room, a large wood desk loaded with folders that I very much hope do not represent unsolved cases, cover most of the top. A man large enough to be in proportion with the room sits behind the desk. He stands to greet us.

"Gentlemen, I wish I could welcome you to our country under different circumstances. I am Peter Salvidar, commissioner of the police."

I shake his hand. "I'm Holden Ashford. This is my friend, Thomas Franklin."

"Please, sit down."

I'd rather stand, but, out of respect, do as he asks. "Do you have any news of my wife?" I ask quickly, unable to waste another second on politeness.

"I am very sorry. But we still have no information as to her whereabouts or Mr. Bartley's. I wish I could tell you differently."

My heart drops instantly, and I'm glad I'm sitting after all. "You know nothing at all about who might have done this?" I ask.

He looks at me for several long moments, and I suddenly see that he is struggling with whether or not to say more.

"Mr. Salvidar, if you know anything that might help us find my wife, please, I'm begging you to tell me."

He draws in a deep breath, and then says, "I do not want to crush your hopes, Mr. Ashford. That is my hesitation in relaying our suspicions of who is possibly behind your wife's abduction—and Mr. Bartley also."

My expression must accomplish what my words did not. He shakes his head a little and says, "A source has provided us with information that leads us to believe your wife and Mr. Bartley might have been abducted for ransom by a drug ring thought to have been altogether extinguished almost two years ago. It might be that some former members of its factions have decided to renew their efforts but are in need of capital. Your wife and friend might have provided that opportunity."

I can barely absorb what he has just said and am still trying to do so when Thomas says, "What can we do?"

"I am afraid there is nothing to do except wait. For more information. Or for them to somehow slip up."

"I don't know how we can possibly do that," I say, my voice hoarse with emotion.

"I wish that I had something better to offer you," he says. "I truly do."

And I believe him.

♪

THE COMMISSIONER RECOMMENDS a nearby hotel and arranges for one of his uniformed police officers to drive us there. He promises to call my cell the moment he learns anything further.

The hotel only has one room available, but we take it anyway since it has two double beds. I don't imagine we'll be doing a lot of sleeping though.

"We've no sooner closed the door to the room and thrown our backpacks on the bed than Thomas looks at me and says, "We can't just sit here and wait for them to call."

"Agreed," I say. " Should we go to the orphanage?"

"Sounds like as good a place to start as any," I say and pull the taxi driver's card out of my pocket.

♪

CeCe

IN MY REAL life, time seems to go by so fast that I'm constantly astonished by the disappearance of one week into another.

That is not true for the passing of time here in this dark room where Jacob and I are locked away against our will.

"Do you think a person could lose their sanity after a while?" I ask, looking at Jacob's face, even as I wonder if I can actually see the outline of his features, or if I am envisioning them from memory.

"Only if you let yourself start to think about it."

"How can we not think about it?" I ask.

"By focusing on the eventual outcome."

"I'm not sure I can make my brain do that."

"Listen," he says, angling his knees toward mine. "Close your eyes and think about a time when you were truly happy. When it seemed as if life could not get any better. Are you?"

"What?"

"Going there?"

I lean my head against the wall behind us, squeezing my eyes shut and letting my thoughts take their own course. For a few moments, I see nothing except blankness. I wait, not saying anything, and then, out of nowhere, I see Holden and me, sitting on the hood of Thomas's truck, looking out beyond us at a beautiful green pasture where contented cows graze. And I feel him lean in close, pressing his mouth to mine.

Warmth cascades through me as I relive the excitement of that moment and how it had felt like the beginning of everything for me. And how I had somehow known that I wasn't supposed to end up in Nashville for music alone. I was supposed to be there so that Holden and I could find each other.

Tears slip through my closed lashes and slide silently down my cheeks.

"Are you crying?" Jacob asks softly.

"A little," I admit.

"I didn't mean to make you do that."

"I know. I can't help it."

"What are you thinking?"

"Honestly?"

"Of course."

"That my husband is the best thing to ever happen to me."

Jacob is quiet for a few moments, and then he says, "I feel sure he would say the same about you. He'd be a fool not to."

"I'm sorry."

"For what?"

"I don't know," I say, not sure how to go on without sounding like I have a big opinion of myself.

"Look. Don't feel bad, CeCe. I knew you were married. Maybe God took notice of my arrogance and decided to give me this knock upside the head."

Laughter bubbles out of me, even though it seems astonishingly inappropriate.

"I might have needed it," he says, the words self-deprecating.

"No," I say. "I don't think God works like that."

"How do you think he works?"

"I guess I think he lets us run into walls once in a while, but I don't think he throws lightning bolts down after us."

"Then maybe this is my wall."

"I know you haven't asked for my opinion, but do you know what I really think?"

"What?"

"That you're lonely. And maybe you're a little tired of the superficial, shallow stuff. But at the same time, you're scared of letting someone into your life. I mean really letting them in."

He's quiet for so long that I'm sure I've overstepped my bounds.

But then he says, "No wonder you're so good at writing songs. You see way more than you let on."

"Maybe I just recognize things I've felt myself," I say.

"I owe you an apology," Jacob says, "and Holden too."

"How about we help you meet a nice girl?" I ask.

"I think God broke the mold after you," he says.

"Nope. And I look forward to proving it to you."

"I'm going to hold you to that."

"Just as soon as we get out of here," I say.

He puts his hand over mine. I turn it up so that our palms are facing, and then I slip my fingers through his, holding onto him as he is holding onto me.

♪

Holden

THE ORPHANAGE isn't what I was expecting.

Although now that the taxi is coming to a stop outside it, I'm not exactly sure what I had imagined.

The building itself is two stories with wide, tall windows. The exterior is whitewashed. Red and yellow flowers fill rectangular boxes beneath the first-floor windows.

"I expected something a lot more dreary," Thomas says, as I pay the driver and we slide out of the back seat.

"Yeah," I say, "me too."

The main door at the front of the building opens, and a very tall, thin woman walks toward us. Her hair is pulled back into a bun, and her navy dress and low heels give her a distinct air of serious sensibility.

Approaching, she says, "I'm Mrs. Castellanos. You are Mr. Ashford?"

"Holden, ma'am. And this is my friend, Thomas Franklin."

"I am so very sorry for what has happened," she says, shaking her head. "I understand you have just come from the police commissioner's office. They have no news at all?"

"No," I say, finding the word hard to get out. "Would you mind if we ask you some questions though?"

"Of course not," she says. "Please, follow me inside."

She turns to lead the way, but before we reach the door, it opens. A young woman with long, dark hair walks out, at least a dozen toddler-age children following her in single file.

I stare. I can't help it. Neither can Thomas. It's a beautiful sight, the parade of little children following the woman to the play ground.

"Do they all live here?" I ask, looking at Mrs. Castellanos.

"Yes," she says. "Along with eleven other groups. We have 130 children in total."

I glance back at the playground where the children are now playing quietly. For toddlers, it seems odd that they aren't laughing and running around.

I think about what CeCe must have felt at seeing them, and I suddenly feel like the most selfish bastard in the world.

"Let's go to my office," Mrs. Castellanos says.

We follow her inside the building and down a long hall to her office. She closes the door behind us and offers us each a chair at the front of her desk. I don't want to sit but do so out of politeness.

She folds her hands on top of the desk and looks at me with sympathetic eyes. "I am very sorry for what you are going through."

"I just want to find my wife," I say, hearing the rasp in my voice.

"I wish I could tell you something that might help, but this thing that has happened is so far out of my—"

"I understand," I say, not wanting to make her feel guilty. "But the police seem to have no leads. Can you think of anyone who might have seen them here? Known about their visit?"

She considers my questions, shaking her head a little when she answers with, "Beyond the people who work here, no. And they all have my complete trust."

Her answer is an immediate closed door. "I'm sorry," I say. "I didn't mean to offend you, ma'am."

"It's okay," she says quickly. "I can only imagine how devastated you must be. But I have to believe they will be found. I choose to believe this."

Her confidence should be reassuring, but somehow, it isn't. "Do you mind if we look around the building, Mrs. Castellanos?"

For a flash of a second, I see something unidentifiable in her eyes. As if she might want to question my reason for doing so. But as quickly as it appears, it's gone, and she says, "Of course, you may. We do ask that you not enter the rooms where the children are."

"Sure," I say.

She shakes my hand and then Thomas's. We leave the office, and once the door closes behind us, Thomas says, "Getting a weird vibe, man. You?"

"Not sure what to think," I say.

We follow the hall to the main entrance and step outside into the courtyard. The sun is strong, the sky a vivid blue. I close my eyes for a moment and try to get a handle on my jumbled thoughts.

"Let's take a walk around the building," Thomas says.

I follow him down the stairs and to the right. The playground is just ahead. I see the same group of children wandering quietly from the monkey bars to the seesaw to the swing set.

We stop short of the fence, both of us watching them.

"It's not right," Thomas says.

"I know. Children aren't that subdued, are they?"

"Not when they have a family to love them," he says.

The woman watching over the children looks up at us, then glances quickly away.

We continue around the building, neither of us talking now. A young guy pulls weeds from the rock surrounding the bushes along the side of the building.

He glances up at us, nods politely, and goes back to his work. We're a few strides away from him when I stop, walking up to him before I say, "Excuse me?"

He leans back, squinting at the sun behind me. "Yes?"

"I was wondering if I might ask you some questions," I say. "I'm—"

"I know who you are," he says abruptly. "Your wife is missing."

"Yes," I say. "Did you see her when she was here?"

He nods. "With the man. Mr. Bartley."

"When was the last time you saw them?" Thomas asks.

"The last afternoon they were here."

"Did you notice anything different?" I ask. "Anything that you might have questioned?"

He shakes his head. "They seemed happy to be here. And they obviously liked each other." And then he says, "Sorry."

It is the last thing I should be feeling, but the words hit my heart like the tip of a knife. I force myself to ignore the stab and say, "Do you remember anyone different visiting the orphanage in the past couple of days?"

"I haven't noticed anyone but the regular people. A delivery truck. The doctor came yesterday, I believe."

"Okay. Thanks," Thomas says, putting a hand behind my arm as he adds, "We appreciate your help."

He starts to walk away then, and I follow him reluctantly. We're at the far corner of the building, out of hearing range, when he looks at me and says, "That definitely didn't feel right."

"No, it didn't. But why?"

"I don't know," Thomas says. "But I'd like to talk to the woman on the playground with the children. I have a feeling she might know something."

"And?"

"You wait right here," he says. "While I go over and break out the Franklin charm."

"Why am I thinking this isn't a good idea?"

"I might be rusty, but I've still got it."

And he leaves me standing there, hoping he's right.

♪

CeCe

I HAVE ALWAYS thought that waiting was the worst part of any impending bad news.

This is no different. Sitting here on this cold, concrete floor, waiting for the door to open again has stretched my anxiety to a level beyond anything I've ever experienced.

Jacob and I stopped talking several hours ago. The silence seems preferable to the small talk neither of us feels like making.

A noise at the door brings Jacob instantly to his feet. "Who is it?" he yells out.

Before he can get across the room, the door opens a few inches. Another package slides across the floor, stopping just in front of him.

The door slams shut again, followed by the clank of a bolt sliding into place on the other side. I now truly hate that sound.

Jacob bends to pick up the package, tearing the seal open. He pulls out a very basic-looking cell phone. He walks back over to sit down next to me.

"Is it working?" I ask.

He taps the screen, and it lights up. "Apparently."

I take the package from his hand and look inside. "There's a note."

"What does it say?"

I remove the paper and unfold it, scanning the words before saying, "They want you to make the call now. It says push the number two and the call will go through."

He takes the paper from my hand, reading it for himself. He looks up at me and says, "They want me to transfer one million dollars into an account that's been opened in my name here."

"It's so much," I say, newly stricken by the amount.

"What if the bank questions it?" Jacob asks, leaning his head against the wall and closing his eyes. "What if they won't do it?"

"Then whatever happens won't be your fault," I say.

"I'm sorry, CeCe," Jacob says.

"For what?"

"Getting you into this."

"Don't do that," I say. "You're not to blame."

"I'm to blame for you being here."

I put my hand on his. "Let's just do what they're asking."

He nods once, takes a deep breath and hits the two on the phone.

♪

Holden

I CALL THE number on the card the taxi driver had given me, and he picks us up at the front of the building.

"Back into town, sir?" he asks, looking at me in the rearview mirror.

"Yes, but could you pull over on the other side of the gate? We'd like to wait for someone."

"Of course," he says, and if he's curious, he doesn't let us see it."

This is Thomas's idea. The Franklin charm had apparently failed, and the young woman had refused to look him in the eyes as she quickly hurried the children back into the orphanage building.

"Why would she not want to talk to me?" he asks now, as if trying to justify our stakeout.

"It doesn't have to mean she knows something," I say.

"No, but it seems strange. Agree?"

"Yeah," I say because it does.

We wait for nearly two hours before the gate opens, and the young woman drives through in a small economy car.

Our driver has been napping for the past hour or so, and Thomas shakes his shoulder, saying, "Wake up! We need to follow that car."

The driver bolts up in his seat, starting the car engine, and jerking it into gear.

"Hold back a moment," I say. "We don't want her to know we're following her."

"Okay," the driver says. "But I have to tell you this will be extra."

"No problem," I say. "If you get us to where she's going without letting her spot us, I'll double the extra."

The driver looks in the rearview mirror and smiles at me. "Incognito it is."

♪

75

CeCe

I WATCH JACOB'S face the entire time he's on the phone. His voice is completely even as he requests the transfer from his account in the United States to the account he has supposedly opened here in Belize.

I'm actually a little shocked by how convincing he is. I'm suddenly glad I'm not the one having to make this call. I have no doubt that I would totally fail at pulling it off.

The call goes on for several minutes, with Jacob supplying yes and no answers in nearly equal proportion. But then an anxious look clouds his face, and I notice him clench his left fist.

Fear surges up through me, and I'm holding my breath when he finally clicks off the call and puts down the phone.

"What is it?" I ask, my voice barely audible.

"Because of the amount, they can't complete the transfer without confirming it with an official at the bank here."

My heart drops instantly. "They're not going to do it, are they?"

Jacob drops his head against the wall behind us, staring up at the ceiling. "It was a lame-ass plan. Clearly, whoever is behind this isn't very sophisticated when it comes to collecting a ransom."

"What do we do now?" I ask, hating the feeling of helplessness raining down on me.

"Well," he says, "if it doesn't go through, I'm assuming they'll come back here to kill us."

"Or they could just leave us here to die."

"I like my scenario better," he says.

"Why?"

"Because when they do, I plan to be ready for them."

♪

Holden

WE FOLLOW THE car at least ten miles before it turns right onto a winding, smaller road.

The driver hangs back a bit, and the car rounds a curve out of sight when Thomas says, "Let's not lose her, man."

The driver hits the accelerator, and within thirty seconds, the car is in sight again. He looks in the rearview mirror at us, shaking his head a little when he says, "I do not need to know what your purpose is, but I think you should know this is an area known for a lot of drug arrests. Sketchy, I believe is your word."

"That's not cool, Holden," Thomas says, looking at me with worry in his eyes. "We could get into some bad stuff."

"You're right, but something is telling me we can't turn back now."

The driver raises his shoulders and says, "Turn around or keep going?"

"Keep going," I say, and he does.

We trail as far behind the car as we can without completely losing sight of it. Just when I think she's never going to stop, her right blinker comes on, and she slows to turn.

"Don't let her see us," I say again, and the driver hangs back a bit more. The road is obviously a driveway, part gravel, part dirt.

"We can't just pull up behind her," Thomas says.

Realizing he's right, I look at the driver and say, "Could you wait here for us again?"

He shrugs. "Of course, but the meter will be very high."

"That's okay. Just don't go anywhere."

The sun is starting to slide down against the horizon as Thomas and I slide from the back seat.

"Any idea what we're getting into here, brother?" Thomas asks.

"None," I say.

"Nothing better than a well-laid plan."

"Wish we had time to make one," I say and take off running down the rutted road. I hear Thomas behind me. We run a quarter mile or so before spotting a small, run-down looking house just ahead.

Chickens roam the muddy yard, pecking intently. A dog is tied at one corner of the porch. He's sitting up, but his eyes are closed, as if he's napping on the job.

The young woman gets out of the car, walks up a set of dilapidated steps and into the house.

"What do we do now?" Thomas asks.

"We need to get close enough to see if we can hear anything."

"Did you notice the very large German shepherd who might object to that?"

"I was hoping you could work your magic with him while I eavesdrop."

"Magic? What magic?"

"The kind you used with Brownie."

"That involved food as a bribe. I don't have any food."

"Thomas—"

"All right, all right," he says. "I'll figure something out. But you'd better be fast."

"I'll go to the left side of the house, and if I can't hear anything, circle the back to the right side."

"Is this supposed to represent a plan?"

"It's all we've got," I say. "Just think dog whisperer."

Thomas rolls his eyes, but says, "Well, then, let's do it."

I go left. He goes right. I'm running. Thomas attempts more of a stroll for his dog-wooing effort.

Knee-high weeds pose as a yard at the side of the house. I leap through, hoping there are no snakes using them for cover.

The first window is closed, but I can see that the next one is raised. A flimsy curtain flaps with the breeze.

I edge along the concrete block wall of the house, stopping just beside the window. I can hear voices, although they're muffled. I'm guessing they're coming from the front of the house. I know I'm taking a risk, but I grab a quick glance inside the room. Seeing no one, I raise the wood window far enough to climb inside.

The good news is I don't hear the dog barking, so Thomas must be having luck with his Cesar Millan impression.

The room is tiny, a single bed with dirty sheets its only feature. I climb through the window and manage to quietly drop onto the floor. The voices are louder now. They're speaking in accented english, and it takes a few moments for my ear to adjust enough to understand.

"There is no choice now," a deep male voice throws out.

"There is always a choice." This from a woman. I'm assuming the one from the orphanage.

"We cannot walk away empty-handed after everything we've done." Another man, and he sounds angry.

"You said the transfer would be a sure thing if he made the call himself." The woman's words are now sharp and accusing.

"I had every reason to think that it would."

"Do you know what the prison sentence is for kidnapping?" the woman asks, venom now coating each word. I try to synch this version of her with the one on the playground and can't make the connection.

My heart is suddenly pounding so hard that I can barely force myself to think. I lean my head back and focus on hearing every word they say.

"We could wait until morning and let him try one more call," the more reasonable sounding man says.

"It is too great a risk," the woman says. "I will not go to prison because of your incompetence. Take care of the problem tonight. When I come back tomorrow, I want to hear that there will be no sign that any of this ever happened."

"You want us to kill them?" one of the men asks quietly.

"If you do not, and we are caught, I will make sure the judge knows that you both coerced me into taking part, and that I feared for my life if I did not go along with you."

The only thing that follows her statement is silence. A hinge squeaks. A door opens and slams, followed by footsteps across the porch.

I'm overcome with the urge to tear into the other room and beat the hell out of both men until they tell me where they're keeping CeCe and Jacob. I force myself to take a breath and wait, hoping they'll say more.

"Man, that was never in the plan."

"Don't act like you didn't think something could go wrong. We all knew going in that it could."

"Kidnapping is one thing. Murder is another altogether."

"If you get caught. I'm not planning on getting caught."

"So what? We just walk in there and shoot them?"

"You have any other suggestions?" the gruff-voiced man asks, heavy on the sarcasm.

"Let them go?"

"So you want to go to prison?"

"No, but I can't take part in this."

"Then I'll do it myself, chicken shit."

I hear the sound of a chair scraping against the floor, followed by heavy footsteps and the door opening.

"Wait!"

The other man is running after him now, and I hear him say, "What will you do with their bodies? What if they're found?"

"They won't be. I'll make sure of it."

I'm acting on nothing but adrenaline now, heading for the window and climbing back out. I trip as I hit the ground, stumble and then get up, running for the front of the house and shouting, "Thomas! Two at the front!"

I'm praying that we get there at the same time, and sure enough, Thomas is rounding the other corner of the house just as I reach the front.

"Get the one closest to you!" I yell.

For a second, both men are clearly paralyzed by surprise. They stand side by side, frozen, and then, all of a sudden, they're both running, off the porch and across the dirt-covered yard. Chickens squawk and fly upward in all directions.

I'm after the bigger guy, and he can run way faster than appearances would lead you to believe. But he is not, NOT, getting away from me. I reach for his shirt, grab fabric, and it rips. He stumbles, hits the ground and rolls. Then he's on his feet again, heading for the gravel road just out from the house.

My lungs are beginning to scream, but I run with every ounce of strength I have inside me. Because I know if I let him get away, I will never see my wife again.

♪

Holden

I TAKE HIM down in a full body tackle. It's like trying to ground a tractor-trailer while it's flying down the Interstate at sixty miles per hour.

He hits the dirt with a belly yell of rage. If I don't somehow manage to hold him down, he's going to kill me. No doubt about it.

I ram a knee in his midsection and aim a right hook to his jaw. Stunned, he stares up at me for a moment, and then his eyes cloud with a fresh wave of rage.

And all of a sudden, it's like wrestling an alligator. His whole body writhes in fury. He flips me backward, and I land on my side, the breath whooshing from my lungs.

I don't give myself time to think about any of it. I lunge for him again, and we're rolling across the gravel, slinging punches. The rocks dig into my arms and back. I land an elbow in his chest. He slams a fist into my cheek. We're both cursing, and then I manage to jam my knee straight between his legs.

He howls. The fight leaves him altogether. He curls up in a ball and curses some more.

I roll away from him, trying to get my breath just as I hear footsteps running toward us.

"Are you okay?" It's Thomas, and I hear the frantic note in his voice.

"Yeah," I manage to grunt, my arms wrapped around my stomach.

"Where's the other guy?"

"I set the dog free and tied him up with the chain."

The answer is so vintage Thomas that I almost laugh. But then I notice alligator man beginning to revive, and there's no way I'm letting him get on his feet again.

I slam him back flat to the ground, my elbow at his throat. "You're going to tell me right now, in this exact moment, where my wife and Jacob Bartley are, or I swear, I will wrap my hands around your neck and choke every last breath from your body."

The guy's eyes are wild with fury, hatred, and something so vile I'm not sure I want to identify it. But I can see instantly that he believes me.

"You can take his word for it," Thomas says, looking down at the man with disgust. "Tell him where she is, or you're history."

"Yeah, and what do I get out of it?" he rasps through gritted teeth.

"You get to live," I say.

♪

CeCe

TIME NO LONGER exists in any order. I have no idea whether it is morning. Or night. Or the middle of the day.

Jacob has been standing by the door for hours. He won't sit, won't come back over here with me. The only thing he will say is that the only chance we have is for him to take them at the door.

He's certain they are coming for us. While I'm thinking they'd be far better off just to leave us here. By the time someone finds us, we'll be dead and unable to reveal anything that might incriminate our kidnappers.

And so we've waited in a silence that has started to feel deafeningly loud.

When I hear the footsteps outside, I am sure I've dreamed them. But then there's a bang, like someone has been shoved into the door. I try to see Jacob's face in the dim light, but I can only make out his shadow, and I know that he is ready.

The bar on the other side lifts. The hinge creaks, and the door swings open.

I see a large figure being shoved inside. And then everything goes crazy at once. The person in front hits the floor and rolls.

And then Jacob goes for the second figure, ramming into him like a crane about to take down a building.

There's rolling and tumbling. I see someone else fumble into the room, and then I hear, "CeCe!"

It's only then that I realize it's Holden on the floor with Jacob.

"Holden! Jacob, stop! Please, stop!"

Both figures go instantly still.

And then I hear Jacob say, "Shit! Holden?"

I'm on my feet then, stumbling across the dark room toward the two of them. I'm right beside them before I can actually see Holden's face. I'm crying so hard I can't breathe.

He grabs me by the waist and lifts me into the air, hugging me so tight I can't get any words out.

"CeCe," he says, his face against my neck. "CeCe."

His voice breaks on my name, and I instantly know the agony I have caused him.

"Hang on, man, she needs to breathe!"

I realize it's Thomas at the door, and now I'm crying even harder.

Thomas walks in, leans over and says, "Jacob?"

"Yeah," he says on a moan. "I've never been so glad to see the cavalry."

"Country boys know how to rock and roll," Thomas says.

"Damn straight," Jacob agrees. "Damn straight."

♪

CeCe

WE'RE IN A taxi headed for the police station. I'm in the back between Holden and Thomas. Jacob is in front with the driver.

Thomas locked the two men apparently responsible for our kidnapping in the same room where we'd spent the past couple of days. I have to admit I hadn't felt an ounce of pity when the metal lock slammed into place.

I've had my face tucked in Holden's shoulder since the moment we got in the car, and all I can think to say is, "I'm sorry. I'm so sorry."

"Shh, baby," he says, pressing his lips against my hair. "Dear God, I'm just so thankful you're safe. I can't tell you how horrible it's been not knowing where you were. How I was going to find you."

"That was the worst part," I say in a low voice so that only he can hear. "Knowing what you must be going through."

"None of that matters now. All that matters is that you're safe. That I have you back."

"How did you find us?" I ask, shaking my head. "I honestly thought we would never be found."

"I'll tell you everything," he says. "But later, okay? Right now I just want to hold you. For the rest of my life might not be long enough."

And I couldn't agree more. It won't be long enough.

♪

Holden

WE SPEND HOURS at the police station.

First, we wait while the two thugs we left in the prison of their own making are picked up and hauled in.

The police commissioner isn't exactly happy to see us. I guess it's a matter of us making him look bad by going out and solving the crime for him.

But once CeCe and Jacob relay their stories, he has no choice but to pick up from here. An assistant parks us in a waiting room and brings food and water for all of us.

CeCe initially says she doesn't want to eat, but I insist, and she takes a few bites of bread to pacify me.

A detective comes in and asks to question us individually. I'm not happy about separating from CeCe, but she assures me she's okay and that this will be the quickest way to get through with it.

As soon as she walks out the door with the detective, the atmosphere shifts. Jacob looks up at me and says, "I did you wrong, man."

I fold my arms across my chest and stare at him for a few seconds, battling between acknowledging his regret and holding onto my anger. "Yeah," I say. "Glad we're on the same page finally."

Jacob looks down at his hands, shakes his head a little. "It was all me, Holden. Where you're concerned, CeCe never wavered."

Relief floods through my chest, and even though I know I never should have doubted her, it's nice to hear. "Vows actually meant something to the two of us," I say in a low voice.

"I know," he says.

Thomas moves away from the wall he's been leaning against and takes a chair next to me. "I gotta tell you, Jacob. What you're looking for, you're never going to find by taking what isn't yours."

He looks up at Thomas, clear regret in his face. "I know that now. I owe you two my life. I won't ever forget it."

"Hey," Thomas says, "I'm just glad it worked out the way it did. It could have gone in a whole different direction."

"Yeah," I say. "Any number of times. But it didn't. So I think we all ought to consider it a reset and get our personal acts together. I certainly haven't been a perfect husband."

Jacob looks off across the room for a moment, and then back at the two of us. "Thank you. To you both. I hope I'll be able to somehow repay you one day."

"No need for that," Thomas says.

Jacob meets my gaze then. I see the uncertainty there. And I realize he needs to hear it from me. "We're cool, man. We're cool."

♪

CeCe

THE QUESTIONING GOES on for so long that by the time we've all taken our turn, I'm not sure I can hold my eyes open a second longer.

When we're finally free to go, it's two in the morning. We take a taxi to the dock and then the charter boat to the hotel where Jacob and I had been staying. He calls ahead to get a room for Thomas, and, as soon as we arrive, we all pretty much stagger to our own doors.

Holden uses the key we'd retrieved from the front desk, inserts it in the lock and pushes it open. He lets me walk in first, and I flick on the lamp next to the bed.

"It feels like a year since I was last here," I say, not quite meeting his gaze.

"It feels like a year since I left Nashville," he agrees.

We look at each other then, awkwardness hanging between us.

"I feel so in need of a shower," I say.

"Go ahead," he says.

"I'll be fast, so you can have it."

"Take your time."

I duck inside the bathroom, shutting the door behind me. I glance at myself in the mirror, instantly horrified by how I look.

My hair looks as if it hasn't been washed in days. Remnants of whatever makeup I'd been wearing the day we were kidnapped make me look as if I've been socked in the eyes.

Unable to look at myself a second longer, I turn on the shower, strip off my clothes and deliberately toss them in the trash can. I never want to see them again.

The water is still cool when I step under the spray, but I don't mind. All I want is to feel clean again. I reach for the shampoo, pour some into my hands and scrub my scalp until it hurts. I pick up the soap then and suds my face and entire body once and then all over again.

I rinse the shampoo from my hair, put in some conditioner and lean against the tile wall of the shower. It's only then that the tears come, and, once they start, I can't stop them.

Great, heaving sobs rise up from my chest while I finally absorb how close we had come to losing our lives, how Holden and Thomas had risked their own lives to get us out of that place.

I hear the click of the bathroom door, look up as Holden steps inside.

"CeCe?"

"Yeah?" I say from behind the shower's steamy glass.

"Are you okay?"

"Yes. I don't know. I think so."

He walks into the room then, stopping outside the glass enclosure. His eyes are on my face, and then his gaze drops the length of my body.

I don't turn away from him. He's my husband, and there's nothing I want more than for him to join me right now.

I guess it must show in my face because he slowly starts to unbutton his shirt. I follow each button, staring at the width of his beautiful chest as he shrugs out of the shirt and drops it to the floor. His hand goes to his belt buckle. Leather flicks against metal as he pulls the belt from his jeans. Snap and zipper are next. And then he's naked there in front of me. I can't take my eyes off him, and when he opens the door and steps into the shower with me, I've forgotten how to draw air into my lungs.

I place my hand at the center of his chest, splaying my fingers wide. "It feels so wonderful to touch you," I say. "To know that you're here. That you're real. That I'm not going to open my eyes and find that I've imagined it."

"Baby, come here," he says, hooking his arm around my waist and pulling me flush against him. He kisses me then, and the warm spray of the shower rains down on our faces.

At first Holden is gentle, so gentle, his mouth achingly familiar against mine. His hands anchor at my waist, and it isn't long before he's kissing me with the kind of hunger that tells me how much he needs me here in his arms.

So I tell him right back, sliding my arms around his neck and molding myself to him. I have never been more grateful to have him in my life than I am now.

And so I don't know why I'm crying. I taste the salt of my tears on Holden's lips. He pulls back and looks down at me, rubbing a thumb across my cheek.

"What is it, baby?"

I glance down, biting my lip and shaking my head. "I just . . . I can't imagine living without you."

He leans in and kisses me with utter tenderness. "You won't have to. Because I know I can't live without you."

I pick up the soap, rub the bar between my hands and lather his chest, his arms and shoulders. And then the rest of him.

He steps into the spray, and the soap slides from his body. When I finally look up at him, his eyes are dark with desire.

"Will you take me to bed now, Holden?" I ask.

And without a word, he lifts me into his arms and does exactly that.

♪

Holden

I'M AWAKE THE rest of the night. Holding CeCe in my arms while she sleeps. I don't want to close my eyes because I'm afraid if I do, I'll wake up to find I've dreamed the whole thing. That she's not really here with me. Safe.

All I can think about is how easy it is to take what we have for granted. How we get complacent when life is going along smoothly. How we forget to cherish those we love.

But lying here in this bed with this woman I love more than my own life, I will never take any of it for granted again. The sweet scent of her hair. The way she fits in the curve of my arm, as if it's exactly where she was made to be.

One thing is completely clear to me now. Accomplishment, fame, material things—none of it means anything if you don't have the one you're meant to be with. Those things are little more than balloons without air if love doesn't breathe life into them.

Sometime just after sunrise, CeCe stirs, moves her cheek on my chest. I rub the back of her hair, kiss her forehead.

"Are you awake?" she asks in a sleepy voice.

"Yeah," I say. "Why don't you try to sleep some more?"

She's quiet for a few moments, and then says, "I dreamed about her."

"Who, hon?"

"Giovanna. The baby."

"You did?"

She nods, silent again for a few moments, and then, "I dreamed we adopted her. That we brought her home with us and got her the surgery she needed."

"And she was okay?" I ask.

CeCe nods, running her hand across my stomach.

We're quiet again. We'd left the window cracked a bit, and I hear the gentle lap of the ocean against the sandy shore just outside the room.

"Well," I say after a while, "I guess the two of us have already proven that dreams can come true."

CeCe raises up on one elbow, looks down at me with a blend of surprise and question in her eyes. "What are you saying, Holden?"

"A little baby girl needs a family to love her. And we're a family with a lot of love to give."

Tears instantly well in her eyes and slip down her cheeks. "What did I ever do to deserve you?"

I lean in and kiss her softly. I finally lean back, saying, "Maybe it's not so much that we deserve love, but that when we're lucky enough to have it, we ought to share it."

"It won't be easy," she says softly.

"Nothing worthwhile ever is," I say. "So we'll take it one step at a time."

"Starting with going to the hospital this morning to see her?"

"Starting with that," I say.

And it's then that my wife wraps her arms tightly around me. Through the open window, a single palm tree sways in the early morning breeze. Just beyond, we watch the sun rise, bright, promising, forever hopeful.

♪

Thirteen Months Later

CeCe

A COUPLE OF years ago, I remember standing in line at the grocery store—Whole Foods in Nashville, I think. The clerk was pregnant. Very. The woman in front of me was chatting with her about the baby's due date.

"When are you expecting?" the customer asked.

"A week or so from now," the cashier behind the register had said without taking her eyes off the items she continued to scan.

The customer seemed not to notice that the young woman didn't appear to want to talk about it. So she continued asking questions.

"Is this your first baby?"

"No. It's not."

"How wonderful. How many will this make?"

"Two."

"Will they be close in age?"

"Yes."

"You must be so excited."

"Worried is probably closer to it," the cashier admitted.

The woman asking the questions looked immediately concerned. "Oh. I hope everything is okay."

The cashier shrugged and said, "I just don't see how it will be possible to love the second child as much as I love the first. That doesn't really seem fair, does it? Bringing a life into the world if you aren't sure you have enough love in you to go around?"

By now, the woman asking all the questions pressed her lips together, as if she had no intention of giving in to the curiosity that had gotten her to this awkward point. "Well," she'd said, clearly in disagreement as she'd grabbed her bags and walked away with a disapproving, "Good luck to you."

The young cashier looked up at me as if she'd expected me to continue with the implied criticism. But I simply paid for my items and left the store.

Except that I'd thought about what she said for a long time after that. Did people have a cap on their capacity to feel and give love? Some kind of perceived limit? If you thought you'd already received an abundance of love in your life and you felt that love in return, was it not possible to love beyond that?

Until Giovanna, I hadn't really known the answer to that question. In Holden, I knew I had been given extraordinary love and felt that love in return. Maybe some part of me had wondered if that young mother in the grocery store was right. Maybe we only have so much love to give.

But I know now the absolute falsity of this.

What I know now is that love doesn't have dimensions or boundaries or the inability to grow.

Love has roots, and if it were confined to the earth, those roots would reach to its very center. Love is fertile beyond any human capacity to define.

My love for Holden, a love I wouldn't have believed possible of becoming something beyond what I already know it to be, has transformed yet again. Watching him with Giovanna, seeing the father he is to her, fills me with a love I have no words to describe.

It's been almost a year since we brought her home from Belize. A year of watching her grow, witnessing the light in her eyes when she sees one of us coming to pick her up. Hearing her laugh when Hank Junior nudges her toes with his wet nose. A year so full of gratitude and happiness that I have often found myself feeling guilty for my blessings.

How is it possible for one person to know the kind of love I have in my life? A husband I adore, a daughter we both love with all our hearts.

And maybe it's this question that has me so dreading Giovanna's surgery tomorrow.

We've known it was coming, that it was a matter of waiting

until she was old enough to have it done, but with every day that's passed, my fear of something going wrong has increased its stranglehold.

This morning, I'm sitting in the kitchen, watching her carefully choose which piece of cereal she wants to eat next, picking up first one, then another, until she finally settles on the perfect choice, waving it at me for approval before popping it in her mouth.

"That one looked delicious," I say. She picks up another piece and offers it to me. I take it, saying, "So, so good."

She laughs at this, kicking her feet against the footrest of the high chair.

Holden walks in the kitchen just then, dropping a kiss on my cheek and then a matching one on Giovanna's. "My two favorite girls starting breakfast without me, I see."

Giovanna raises her arms for him to pick her up. "Are you done, Gigi angel?" he asks.

She nods, saying, "Da-da."

He lifts her out of the chair, whirling her around, before settling her in the curve of his arm. She giggles, looking up at him with wide, adoring brown eyes.

Holden loops an arm around my waist and pulls me against him, Giovanna tucked between us. "Gigi sandwich," he says, and she giggles at the familiar game.

I kiss the back of her head, letting myself meet Holden's warm gaze. I try to blink away the worry I know he will see in my eyes, but I'm not successful because he runs his hand across the center of my back and says, "Everything is going to be okay."

I rest my forehead against his shoulder, breathing in Giovanna's sweet baby scent. "I know," I say.

"We can't let ourselves think anything other than that," he says, pressing his lips against my hair.

"I'm terrified," I say.

"We've done everything we can to find the best doctor for her.

And Dr. Moses has given us every reassurance. That's where we have to keep our focus, babe."

I nod against his chest, putting my hand on Giovanna's little round leg and rubbing my thumb against her soft skin. "I would give anything if I could take her place."

"So would I."

And I know it's true. We both would.

"It's hard to imagine now that we were ever without her," I say.

He nods, and I sense that he doesn't trust himself to speak.

"Sometimes, I feel so guilty, Holden."

"Why?" he asks softly.

"Because I have you. And Giovanna. How can I deserve so much?"

He rubs his thumb across my jawline, looking down into my eyes. "I don't think we're supposed to feel guilty for being loved and having love. I do think we're supposed to be grateful for it and to share it with others. And maybe it's not so much what you get in this world as what you give back."

I nod, pressing my cheek to his chest, my hand still on Giovanna's leg. He's right, and we've both become more and more mindful of this since adopting our precious girl. It's become so clear to us that adoption is a gift we can share with others, especially the message of what a mutual blessing it is for both parents and child.

"Hopefully, the surgery will all be over by this time tomorrow."

I slip my arm around his waist, and put the other around Giovanna, hugging them both to me. "Do you ever wonder how all of this happened?"

"Sometimes. But then I remind myself there's only one way any of it could have happened. God's plan, not ours."

Truly, there's no other explanation for it. I know this as well as Holden does. The doors that were opened for us regarding Giovanna's adoption. The hearts that were softened by our experience in Belize and by our desire to get Giovanna the medical intervention she needed. I don't think any of it would ever have happened had Jacob and I not been kidnapped, and Holden and Thomas ended up helping the authorities put away the drug dealers who held us hostage.

"It's incredible that we have her, isn't it?" I say.

"It is," Holden says. "And she's going to be okay, our GiGi."

His voice soothes my raw nerves, as only it can do. Holden is my rock, the place I can go when nothing in this world makes sense. In his arms, I'm somehow able to push reset and get myself back to a place of believing everything will be all right.

This morning is no different. I hold onto him, knowing he'll get us through the sea of fear and worry we will have to navigate in the next twenty-four hours.

And I'm thankful for him. So thankful. "I love you so much, Holden."

"I love you too. We'll get through this. We will."

I know I shouldn't cry. But I can't stop myself. I'm so scared for Giovanna. Scared that she'll feel pain. Scared that something will go wrong. Scared of losing her.

Holden hugs me tighter against him, whispering *shhh* against my ear. There it is. My anchor. My harbor in the storm. This man who is my other half. I hold onto him as he holds onto me. And I never want to let go.

♪

Holden

I PULL UP in front of Thomas and Lila's house at just after one o'clock to drop off Hank Junior and Patsy. They're going to stay here the next few days.

Thomas and Brownie walk out to greet us, Hank and Patsy eager to get out of the car as soon as they see the other dog. All three do a reintroduction of sniffing and tail wagging in the grass next to the driveway as Thomas walks over and claps me on the shoulder.

"Hey, man," he says. "How are you?"

I hear the worry behind the question, and, because it's Thomas, let down my guard a bit. "I've been better."

"We've just got to get tomorrow behind us," he says in a compassionate voice. "She's going to be okay, Holden."

I nod, suddenly not trusting myself to speak.

"How's CeCe?" he asks.

"Holding it together. Or maybe we're holding each other together."

"I didn't sleep much last night," Thomas admits. "So I can't even imagine how you two are passing the hours."

We both walk into the yard where the dogs are now playing full out, even little old Patsy chasing after Brownie and Hank and giving it her best.

"Be nice to have their life sometimes, wouldn't it?" Thomas asks.

I shove my hands in the pockets of my jeans and shrug. "Yeah."

"You remember being a kid and not understanding why grownups were always so stressed?"

"Believe me, now I get it," I say.

Thomas nods in agreement. "My Grandma Franklin was a worrier. When I was around ten, I started to realize that she really couldn't find any joy in something positive that might happen to

101

her because she was already trying to figure out what to dread or worry about next. One time I asked her why she spent so much time thinking about what might happen."

"What did she say?" I ask.

"She said the only way she could feel in control of her life was trying to figure out where the potholes were going to be."

"Trouble is, I don't think you can," I say.

"Me, either. But it's not like they're any big surprise. With the good, you're gonna get the bad now and then. Maybe that's life's way of testing us. Making sure we understand the value of what we have."

"You think we have to fear losing someone before we get how much we love them?"

"To a certain extent, I guess I do think that," he says. "We're human. We start to take things for granted."

"I don't take my family for granted," I say, hearing my own defensiveness.

"I know you don't."

"Sorry," I apologize. "I know what you're saying. You and Lila amaze me every day the way you don't focus on the things that are hard for Lexie but instead see her potential for everything."

"Well, thanks for that, but we just love her. That makes the rest easy."

I look up at Thomas, see the compassion in his eyes and realize, not for the first time, how lucky I am to call him a friend. "Thanks, man. For being there for us. You always are."

"It's not hard, Holden," he says in a slightly unsteady voice. "That's what love does."

♪

CeCe

THE HOSPITAL TERRIFIES me.

Walking through the front doors with Giovanna sleeping against my chest and Holden leading the way, I am overcome with the urge to turn around and run as fast as I can away from this place. Every bad memory I've ever had of hospitals and the events that led to being there washes over me, choking the air from my lungs.

As if he feels my fear, Holden drops back, putting his arm around my shoulders. We walk to the information desk where he tells a woman in a pink hospital smock why we are here.

She smiles sympathetically, her gaze falling across Giovanna and instantly softening. "Follow me," she says. "You'll need to fill out some paperwork."

She leads us down a hallway and stops at a door marked **Check In**. She knocks and then pushes the door open. A woman with dark red hair and pink lipstick looks up at us, recognition lighting her eyes. "Hello," she says. "I'm Sandra. I was expecting you. So nice to meet you both. I'm a big fan."

"Thank you," Holden says.

Sandra stands and waves us toward the chairs in front of her desk. "Please sit down."

The woman in the pink smock leaves, closing the door behind her.

Giovanna starts to stir, and I shift her in my arms, cradling her against my chest.

"She's precious," Sandra says.

I try to smile my thanks, but my lips feel frozen, and I can't force it.

"I know this is a stressful time for you both, so I'll try to make this as brief as possible," she says, sitting down in her chair. "But we do have quite a few documents for you to read and sign."

"Of course," Holden says.

She pulls a file from the top of a small stack at the center of her desk. She opens it and removes the top paper. "If you could both read through this, I'll need your signatures at the bottom on the lines with the yellow X."

Holden places the page between us so that we can read it at the same time. I shift Giovanna in my arms, her head resting on my shoulder. She's not quite asleep but is content to snuggle there.

I force my gaze to the first line and start to read.

It is important to your doctor that you understand and consent to the treatment your doctor is rendering and any surgery your doctor may perform. You should be involved in all decisions concerning the surgical procedure. Sign this form only after you understand the procedure, the risks, the alternatives, the risks associated with the alternatives, and all of your questions have been answered.

My stomach drops, and I feel suddenly sick. I want to stop reading, but I can't, so I go on.

The risks associated with the procedure have been explained to me including, but not limited to, blood loss, transfusion reactions, infection, heart complications, blood clots, loss of or loss of use of body part or other neurological injury or death.

Holden reaches for my hand and clasps it tightly between his. We finish reading the paper, and he signs his name on one line. I switch Giovanna to my left arm and sign my name on the other line.

Sandra takes the paper from us, saying, not without sympathy, "I'm sure everything will be fine. Dr. Jamison is a wonderful surgeon."

I try to nod, but I can't. I put both my arms around our baby and hug her as tightly as I dare.

♪

Holden

IT'S NOT THE FIRST time in my life that I've felt helpless.

I knew this kind of helplessness a year ago when I realized CeCe was missing, and I had no idea how to go about finding her.

But as horrible as that was, this is different.

CeCe and I sit on either side of Giovanna's special hospital bed, each of us stroking her back and legs. She's been asleep for a while, darkness falling hours ago outside the room's narrow window.

Neither of us will sleep tonight, even though I know we should. We will need the strength tomorrow. So I wish we could sleep. It would take some of the awful dread out of these hours before her procedure. But I think we're both afraid to fall asleep, maybe deep down terrified that if we do, we'll have wasted precious time with her.

As soon as the thought runs through my mind, I realize what it means.

That I'm scared to death we will lose her.

That these might be our last hours with her.

CeCe reaches across the bed and takes my hand, squeezing hard, as if she knows what I'm thinking. I squeeze back, and let myself meet her gaze, seeing the pain there and wishing I had the ability to take it away.

"We're going to get through this. Everything will be okay," I say.

She bites her lower lip, her eyes brimming with tears. "It will," she says.

And for the rest of the night, we sit this way, locked together around this tiny girl we love as our very own.

♪

CeCe

JUST BEFORE FIVE-THIRTY a.m., two nurses with a gurney appear at the door.

They roll it quietly inside the room, the one closest to us saying, "It's time for this little sweetie to go upstairs."

Giovanna is awake, lying on her back, her eyes wide and innocent about what the day will hold for her. I take her small hand in mine and say, "Want to go for a ride on the rolling bed, sweetie?"

For a moment, her eyes light up, and then, as if she feels the falseness of my smile, she glances at Holden and starts to cry.

"It's okay, baby," he says. "We'll go with you."

"You can go as far as the operating room doors," one of the nurses says in a kind voice, "but no farther."

Giovanna's bottom lip trembles, and she starts to cry harder.

As if he knows I can't do it, Holden reaches down to lift her from the bed and into his arms, walking over to the gurney where the nurses are waiting. He starts to place her on the white sheets, but she clings to him, her arms tightening around his neck.

I've never seen Holden look so broken, and when he turns to the nurse, his voice wavers as he says, "May I carry her there? Please."

The two women glance at each other, and without saying anything, they both nod. They roll the gurney back out of the room, and we follow them, forcing ourselves to take each and every step down the long hallway to the elevator.

Nothing in my life has ever felt as hard as this.

I want to grab our baby and run from this hospital, but even as the instinct overwhelms me, I know it would be risking her life to do so. She needs this surgery to grow up with a healthy heart, and we have no choice but to take all of the risks so deliberately outlined in the documents we signed yesterday afternoon.

And so I force myself to put one foot in front of the other, to walk beside my husband, my hand on Giovanna's small arm.

We arrive at the operating room doors all too soon. DO NOT ENTER – HOSPITAL PERSONNEL ONLY marks the center of the automated white doors.

"We'll take very good care of her," one of the nurses says to me. I can see in her eyes she is aware of my terror, and I guess she has seen this look many times in the eyes of other parents.

Holden kisses Giovanna's cheek. I lean in and kiss her too, clinging now to Holden's arm because I am afraid my legs will buckle beneath me.

One of the nurses pushes the button to open the doors, and the other reaches to take Giovanna from Holden. She doesn't try to place her on the gurney, but turns quickly to walk into the area where we are not allowed. The other nurse follows her with the empty gurney.

Holden and I stare at the doors as they close in front of us. A gasp of agony slides from my throat, and the room tips before my eyes. Holden reaches for me, pulling me to him, as if he knows I'm going to fall.

"Come on, babe," he says, his voice reflecting the pain I am also feeling. "We have to wait. We'll get through this. We will."

Pressed against his side, I let him lead me to the waiting room.

I'm so relieved to find that it's empty. Holden closes the door behind us, and I fall into his arms, the sobs locked deep inside me finding their way out to drown the silence of the room with fear and heartbreak.

♪

Holden

THOMAS AND LILA arrive at the hospital at just after six-thirty. They walk into the waiting room with a tray of Starbucks coffee and expressions of pained sympathy. Somehow, I know that they understand what we're going through. They've had times of fearing for Lexie, and their empathy is real.

They both hug us hard, pass us each a cup of coffee, and we sit in the straight-back chairs, not even up to small talk.

A half hour or so later, Case and CeCe's mom, Mira, arrive, their faces set with worry. Mira sits down next to CeCe and pulls her into her arms, holding her daughter for a long time.

We spend the next several hours waiting, mostly silent, forcing conversation when the silence becomes too heavy.

At just after ten, a nurse opens the door. "Dr. Moses asked me to let you know that things are going well," she says. "He knows how concerned you are and hoped to give you some relief."

"How much longer?" I ask, unable to keep the impatience from my voice.

"I don't know," she says kindly. "I'll come back as soon as we are able to tell you something more."

I feel guilty for my shortness with her, but before I can apologize, she's already left the room, the door closing behind her with a definitive click.

Thomas puts a hand on my shoulder and squeezes once, as if to say no one blames me for it.

I get up from my chair and walk to the window that looks out over a bustling Nashville, the rest of the world going on as usual, while we wait here with ours on hold.

♪

CeCe

IT'S AFTER TWO o'clock when the telephone in the waiting room rings. Holden answers it, silent for several seconds before saying, "Okay. Thank you."

He puts the phone down and turns to us, saying, "That was someone from the OR. The surgery is finished, and the doctor is on his way up to talk to us."

"Did they say anything else?" I ask, my heart suddenly pounding hard.

"No," he says, walking over to sit back down next to me. He takes my hand, and Mama, sitting on my left, also entwines hers with mine.

Fifteen very long minutes pass before the door opens, and the doctor walks in. He looks tired, and pushes the green surgical cap from his head, as if he has forgotten it was still there.

"Sorry for the long wait," he says. "The procedure took longer than we expected, but I feel very good about the outcome."

"Is she all right?" I ask, my voice barely audible.

"We were able to repair the hole in Giovanna's heart, and I have every reason to believe she will lead a very normal life."

The words sit at the edge of comprehension for several moments, my own fear that he might say something very different preventing me from absorbing them. But then Holden puts his arm around me and pulls me to him, kissing the side of my hair and saying, "She's all right, babe. She's all right."

And now, after all these hours of waiting, I let myself cry. Not from grief. But for joy.

♪

Holden

EVEN AFTER THE doctor tells us the news, we wait another hour before a nurse comes to let us know we can see our daughter. Giovanna will be in the Pediatric Intensive Care Unit (ICU) overnight, so our visits will be limited, and for now, only CeCe and I are allowed in.

Case and Mira, along with Thomas and Lila, all follow us to the ICU on the fifth floor. They wait outside the double doors as we go in.

Her bed is in the far right corner of the room, and a kind-faced nurse leads us over, saying, "She's still very groggy. Don't expect her to respond right now, okay?"

CeCe nods, and I say, "Thank you."

She leaves us alone with Giovanna then, and I think it isn't until I'm able to take in her small body against the white sheets that I can fully believe we haven't lost her.

CeCe takes her tiny hand, leans down and presses her lips against it. "Sweet baby," she says softly. "Thank goodness, you're okay."

She has a tube in her nose, and her tiny mouth is open, her breathing slightly raspy. CeCe smooths her hand across Giovanna's dark hair, and says, "We're here, precious girl. Take all the time you need to feel better."

Her eyes flutter open, and she tries to focus on us. But the medicine lures her back to sleep, and she closes her eyes again.

"She's fine, CeCe," I say, putting a hand on her shoulder and squeezing in reassurance. "It's better if she sleeps now."

"I know." She leans in and kisses Giovanna's forehead. "We're so lucky, Holden."

"We are," I say. And I have never been more grateful for the amazing gift we were given in our daughter than I am at this very moment.

♪

CeCe

LIKE SO MANY things we dread in life, Giovanna's surgery doesn't seem so overwhelming in hindsight.

Three days after the operation, she is eating and wanting to get out of bed and play. She's in a regular room now, and there has been a nearly ceaseless line of visitors since she was moved here from ICU yesterday afternoon.

Holden has gone home to shower, and I'm holding Giovanna on my lap, reading her a story when Mama knocks at the door. She had stayed at the hospital with us last night, leaving this morning to go home and get some rest.

"Hi, honey," she says, slipping into the room and closing the door behind her. She's carrying a pink teddy bear, which she hands to Giovanna who reaches for it with outstretched arms.

Her gurgling sounds of approval and the way she instantly squeezes it to her chest makes Mama smile.

"I thought you might like him," she says. "She's just like you, CeCe. You never saw a stuffed animal that you didn't want."

I smile too, remembering how my bed had eventually been so full of them that there was nowhere for me to sleep. "She does love them," I say.

"She looks wonderful," Mama says, studying Giovanna with the same trying-not-to-be-worried intensity I find myself studying her with.

"I can't believe we actually have this behind us," I say, kissing the side of Giovanna's head.

"I know you've dreaded it so much," Mama says, sitting down on the edge of the bed next to us.

"It seems like a bad dream now," I say. I glance out the window where the sky beyond the hospital is a bright blue. "Time kind of stops when you're in a place like this."

"It does," Mama agrees, "but now you all need to get on with your lives and enjoy the incredible blessing you've been given."

"She is that," I say. "I think I realize now how worried I've been about her since we brought her home. We had this awful 'what-if' hanging over us. What if the doctors couldn't repair her heart?"

"But they did," Mama says, covering my hand with hers.

"I need to focus on that, don't I?"

"Yes," Mama says. "But I know your fear and how hard it is to turn your back on it once you've come face to face with it."

She glances out the window and then meets my gaze, her eyes suddenly darkening with emotion. "The night you were shot. There was a period of time when I thought I was going to lose you, CeCe. Even now, I don't have words to describe what that was like."

"I'm sorry you had to go through that, Mama," I say, hearing the remembered anguish in her voice. And I realize it's only now that I've faced the possibility of losing Giovanna that I understand what she must have felt.

She looks at me with such love that I am newly aware how fortunate I am to have her as my mother. "I love you, Mama."

"I love you too, my sweet girl."

♪

Holden

IT FEELS GOOD to take a shower at home. I stand under the pummeling spray for a long time, letting the hot water pound the tension and worry from my muscles.

Gradually, relief begins to replace the stress, and along with it, gratitude. I have never been more thankful for my life than I am right now. CeCe and Giovanna are my world, and that world has tilted on its axis these past few days.

Suddenly, I'm overcome with the need to express that, to let them both know how much they mean to me. I get out of the shower, pull on jeans and a shirt, and then go downstairs for my guitar.

Even as I pick it up, the melody has unfurled itself to me, the words of the song right behind it. Everything I feel is there, and I have no clearer way to express it.

♪

CeCe

AS SOON AS he hits the last note, I ask him to sing it again.

The door to Giovanna's room is closed, and Holden sings softly, so I'm not worried about disturbing others. With our daughter asleep in the bed next to us, I absorb every word he has written, and when he's again done, I can't hold back my tears.

"It's beautiful, Holden," I say. "So beautiful. Thank you."

He leans over and kisses me softly. I slide my arms around his neck, the guitar still between us. He cups his hand to the side of my face, and we kiss for a good while, the fear that has tentacled our every word, every touch, while we waited for this surgery to be over, gone.

He puts the guitar against the wall and then pulls me onto his lap. I wrap myself around him, and we hold each other tight and hard. No words are necessary. Our hearts hear each other. And understand.

♪

CeCe

HOLDEN INSISTS THAT I go home; let him stay the night.

At first, I hadn't wanted to, but I am so exhausted that fatigue seems to have replaced the blood in my veins. I want to stop at Thomas's and pick up Hank and Patsy, but all I can think of doing right now is collapsing into our bed.

I force myself to take a quick shower and then fall onto the mattress wearing a towel instead of my pajamas.

And for the first time in many, many nights, I sleep.

♪

Holden

SOMETHING WAKES ME.

Daylight is peeking through the narrow window of the hospital room. I lift my head from the chair I've been sleeping in, trying to focus on the sound. I sit up just as I hear it again.

And then I realize it's Giovanna. Whimpering.

I jump to my feet. "Gi. What is it, baby?"

I run my hand across her forehead then, my heart nosediving in my chest.

She is burning up.

♪

Holden

THREE NURSES WORK quickly and efficiently over Giovanna.

I stand to the side, watching helplessly as they add medicine to her IV and listen to her heart with a stethoscope.

The one closest to me, an older woman with sharp blue eyes and white hair says, "We've paged her doctor. He should be here any minute."

"What's wrong?" I ask, trying to keep my voice even, but not succeeding.

"Let's wait for him, Mr. Ashford. I know this is difficult, but we'll need to see what he says before doing anything further."

I take Giovanna's hand between mine, gripping as tightly as I dare. I try not to think about the heat there. I'm torn between the need to call CeCe and the fear of letting go of our child, the thought that holding onto her is the only way I can be sure she won't leave us.

The minutes crawl by, and I'm not sure how long it is before Dr. Moses appears in the doorway. The nurses waiting in the room with us look as relieved as I feel.

"Holden, would you mind waiting outside the room while I have a look at Giovanna? I think it would be the easiest thing."

I stare at him for a moment, wanting to tear into him as much as I have ever wanted to tear into another person. I don't want to leave her even for a second.

But I check the impulse, forcing myself to let reason in. I know he is only doing his job, and I need to let him do whatever he can for her.

I lean over and kiss her cheek, my heart a hard, solid knot in my chest. "Hold on, Gi," I say and then leave the room in quick strides, not letting myself think about anything except reaching the other side of the door.

In the hallway, I lean against the wall and close my eyes tight, sending up a prayer for Giovanna even as I pray that it will be heard.

I pull my phone from my pocket then and do the thing I wish I did not have to do. Destroy altogether the happiness I had seen on my wife's face when she left the hospital last night.

♪

CeCe

I DRIVE WITH deliberate focus, my hands gripping the steering wheel so hard that my fingers are white. I strain to keep my eyes on my lane in the Interstate traffic, afraid if I glance away for even a moment, I'll make a mistake, hit another car, veer off the side of the road and not make it to the hospital in time.

In time for what?

The question is like an electrical shot through my brain. And I don't let myself go beyond that.

Our baby is going to be fine.

Nothing else is even a possibility.

♪

CeCe

BUT AS SOON as I get to the hospital and see the look on Holden's face, I realize that it is not fine.

"Babe," he says and pulls me directly into his arms, squeezing me so tightly against him that I feel as if I am about to pull him back from the edge of a cliff.

"What is it?" I ask, dreading what he is going to tell me almost as much as I have to know.

Holden leans back and looks into my eyes, brushing his hand across my hair. "Dr. Moses . . . he thinks . . ."

He stops there, as if he can't go on.

"Tell me," I say, grabbing his shoulders and forcing him to look at me. "What is it, Holden?"

"She's contracted a staph infection," he says finally. "They're doing another culture now to determine the best antibiotic to use."

The words ping at my comprehension like ice balls on a metal roof, refusing to absorb. "A staph infection?"

"Hopefully, one they can treat quickly," he says, his voice attempting reassurance but not quite succeeding.

"Where is she?" I ask. "Can we see her?"

"The nurse just took her down for a chest x-ray. I don't think they'll be long."

With the words, my composure crumples, and I fall against him, suddenly so overcome with sobs that I cannot breathe.

"Hang on, babe," he says, pulling me into his arms and sealing me to him. "She's strong. She'll fight this."

"What if she can't?"

"She will. She will."

I press my face to his chest and try to smother my crying. It sounds like weakness, like faithlessness, and if Giovanna has to be strong, then so do I. I tell myself this is a test. To prove that we are deserving of her.

I can't fail.

I won't fail.

♪

WHEN DR. MOSES returns to Giovanna's room, I am holding her in my arms, rocking her gently back and forth in the rocking chair by the window. She is asleep, but the look on her tiny face isn't one of rest but exhaustion.

"I'm sorry for the delay," Dr. Moses says, standing next to Holden. "I actually asked the lab to double-check the culture to make sure we make the best decision regarding Giovanna's treatment. We will be adding the medicine to her IV within the next half hour."

"How long before it begins to help her?" Holden asks, his voice raw with emotion.

"I wish I could give you both a definitive answer, but it depends on Giovanna's own immune system and her ability to fight this infection. I would hope to see a difference in the next twenty-four hours."

One day. Twenty-four hours. It sounds like a lifetime from now.

"And, of course," Dr. Moses continues, "we'll be working to control her temperature. I think it would be wise to move her back to ICU as an extra precaution. She will be continually monitored there."

Dr. Moses squeezes my shoulder and then claps his hand on Holden's back. He says nothing more as he turns to walk out the door, but I can feel the heaviness of his distress and sympathy. I know it should be reassuring to have a doctor who cares as much as he does. But it feels as if the current that brought us into the safety of the shore has now washed us back out again. The water is so deep, and I already feel the struggle to stay above the surface.

And so, once the door closes behind Dr. Moses, I cannot hold back the tears welling inside me. Holden squats next to the rocking chair and wraps his arms around me and Giovanna. But for the first time, I feel that he has no more strength than I do, that we will both struggle to endure this wait.

I want to tell him I am here for him, that I understand what he is feeling, that we are far stronger together than we are individually. But I cannot find my voice, cannot muster the strength. All I can do is rest my head on his shoulder and hold our daughter between us, praying that our combined strength will find its way to her.

♪

Holden

ONCE THEY TAKE Giovanna back into the ICU, we are again only allowed to go in to see her a few minutes at a time.

Case and Mira, along with Thomas and Lila, return to the hospital as soon as CeCe calls to let them know what has happened. Mira walks in to the waiting room with fresh tears in her eyes, going to CeCe and pulling her into her arms. I can see that Lila has also been crying as well.

Thomas walks straight over and hugs me without hesitation. He doesn't say anything though, which is completely out of character for him. But just meeting eyes with him, I know he has no idea what to say that would be of any comfort.

Case grabs my shoulder and squeezes hard, his voice gruff when he says, "Y'all are gonna get through this. Just hold on, okay?"

From there, we're a quiet group, each of us sitting silently next to one another, lost in our own thoughts. When the door swings open, I get to my feet, expecting to see Dr. Moses or one of the nurses.

But it's a young woman, holding a notebook under her left arm. A guy who looks as if he's barely out of college is right behind her with an enormous TV camera on his shoulder. I notice immediately that it is already filming.

"What are you doing?" I ask, stepping toward him.

To my surprise, he doesn't back up but continues filming.

The woman raises her hand and says, "We won't take much of your time, Mr. Ashford. I'm Natalie Townsend. We're with *The Insider*. I'm so sorry that your daughter is sick, but I'm sure you must understand how much your fans want to know how she is doing."

It takes a moment for her words to settle into comprehension.

Her presence in this room feels like such an invasion of privacy that it is all I can do not to shove them both out the door.

I guess CeCe must sense this because she is suddenly standing beside me, her hand on my arm. "We're not really in a place where we want to speak publicly," she says to the woman. "Surely you can understand—"

"Actually, I'm afraid I can't," she says, holding the microphone in her right hand a little closer to CeCe. "You've made your fortune from the fans who support your music. Don't you think they have a right to know when something is going on in your life?"

The college camera guy continues his filming, and it is only this that keeps me from lunging at the woman.

I force myself to take a deep breath, fully aware that this is a reporter with an agenda and anything I say in defense of our desire for privacy will be used against us. "Ms. Townsend, do you have children?"

"No," she says. "I don't." Her tone indicates she's not going to be open to my rationale, but I go on anyway. I want to yell at her, make them both the object of the rage inside me.

Instead, I force calm into my voice and say, "If you did, I have to believe you would feel the same way about protecting your child as my wife and I do about protecting ours. We chose a life that involves being in the public eye, but our daughter did not. It's not our right to exploit her illness for any reason, least of all public curiosity."

"Some would call it public sympathy," she disagrees.

"That might be," I say. "But we are her parents, and it's our job to protect her."

"And it's my job to report the news," she says.

"Human tragedy is news to you?"

"We do our best to be respectful," she responds, a defensive note in her voice.

"Taking advantage of people when they're at their most

vulnerable?" I ask in a measured voice. "Like the reporters who were let into the house of those terrorists in California a few months ago? The ones who showed viewers pictures of their young baby, her toys, and the crib she slept in before her parents got themselves shot? That child had nothing to do with her parent's choices. And neither does our child."

I watch the battle play out across the reporter's face. I wait in deliberate silence, realizing I have said everything I know to say.

Finally, she waves a hand at the camera guy and says, "Shut it off, please."

Reluctantly, he does, lowering the front. "Natalie, this isn't your decision to make. We were given a story to cover."

"And I'll answer for the decision," she says firmly.

CeCe walks over then, tucking her arm through mine. "Thank you," she says to Natalie. "It really means a lot to us."

"I might lose my job," she says in a voice no longer hard with determination. "But I had a little sister who developed leukemia when she was eight. I was twelve. I remember how hard it was for our family to see her that way. I can understand how you must want to shield your daughter from further hurt."

"I'm sorry about your sister," CeCe says.

"We had two more years with her before—" She breaks off there, her face clouding with memories.

"I'm so sorry," CeCe says again, this time reaching out to put a hand on her arm.

Natalie nods once and looks at the guy still holding the camera. His expression has softened, and even though I'm sure he isn't in favor of catching it from his boss, he at least appears to understand her decision.

"Good luck to you both," she says, and they leave the room.

Thomas, who has been standing near the window with Lila, Case, and Mira, says, "Well, that's a first."

"Yeah," I say.

"Maybe the lesson here is that everyone can identify with the innocence of children," Thomas says.

"So there's hope for the human race, after all?" I say.

Thomas doesn't look as if he's convinced of it, but offers a reluctant, "Maybe."

♪

CeCe

FOR THE NEXT forty-eight hours, Holden and I are the constants in the waiting room outside the ICU.

Mama, Case, Thomas and Lila come and go, staying as much as they can. Thomas and Lila need to be with Lexie after school, and they are also making sure Hank Junior and Patsy are taken care of. Holden and I take turns going home to shower and change clothes before coming right back. Every time we're allowed to go in to see Giovanna, we do, hopeful with each visit that she will appear stronger.

But it isn't until the beginning of her third day in the unit that I notice a change in her. Her lips, pale and colorless since the infection began, are tinted with their former rose. Standing at the side of her bed, I take her hand and squeeze it between mine, so grateful for this small sign of improvement.

Holden puts his hand on my shoulder, and I feel his hope merge with my own. We both keep our eyes intently on her sweet face, and Holden says, "Gi? Baby, can you hear us?"

Her eyelids tremble slightly, and I feel the breath catch in my throat. "Giovanna? Sweetie?"

Her eyes flicker open then, halfway, close again, and then open wide. She looks at both of us, as if she's trying to focus. I see the moment she recognizes us, the clarity that suddenly darkens her beautiful brown eyes. And then a smile breaks across her face, soft and reassuring.

"Oh, baby," I say, lifting her from the bed into my arms. "Mommy and Daddy are here. You're going to be fine, sweetie. You're going to be fine."

Holden wraps his arms around us both, and here we are again, a family.

♪

Holden

IN THE WEEKS following Giovanna's release from the hospital, CeCe and I barely leave the house, choosing to spend nearly every minute of the day caring for her, witnessing her ever-increasing strength and return to the formerly joyful baby she had been before the surgery.

And as she improves, both CeCe and I start to lose our unspoken fear that something will go wrong again, that the infection will come back, that her heart might not really be repaired. Even so, we're both still tenuous about letting her out of our sight, watching her play with the other children at the park with a fear that she will overdo it, exert too much energy.

One night after Giovanna is asleep, CeCe and I are lying in bed talking about the day. The dogs are asleep at the foot of the bed. I brush my hand across CeCe's hair and say, "I think it's time for us to stop being afraid."

Her head on my chest, she traces a pattern on my collar bone. I have no doubt she knows what I mean when she says, "I want to. Stop, I mean."

"If we keep treating her like she's fragile, she'll grow up thinking there's something wrong with her. That maybe she can't do things other kids do."

"I don't want that."

"Me either. I want her to be carefree, play with other kids without the two of us fretting over her."

"Fretting?" she says in a teasing voice.

"Southernism," I say.

She smiles against my chest. "We have been, haven't we?"

"In our defense, understandably. But we can't keep living as if something might go wrong at any minute."

"It's not right for her. Or for us."

"I know. So what do we do?"

"I think just get back to our regular life. Doing what we do. Writing. Playing. Singing."

"I've actually been missing it," she says.

"Maybe we all are. Thomas stopped by this morning when you were out. He brought up the possibility of doing a tour this summer. All of us. Giovanna, Lila, and Lexie too. A chance to show the girls the country."

"What do you think?" she asks softly.

"I'd like to," I say. "The tour bus is big enough for all of us."

"And the dogs," CeCe says.

"And the dogs," I say, rubbing a hand across her hair.

She tips her head to look at me. "Maybe we could work adoption into the theme of the tour. Maybe show others what a gift it is."

I lean in and kiss her warm mouth. "That's a great idea."

She slips her body across mine, looking down at me with such love that I feel the squeeze of it in my heart.

"Sometimes I still can't believe you're my husband," she says.

I chuckle. "You mean that in a good way or a bad way?"

"A very good way," she says, moving against me. "In fact, I'm thinking maybe we should start trying to give Giovanna a little sister or brother."

"There's a thought," I say, flipping her over so that her body is beneath mine.

She smiles up at me, kisses the corner of my mouth. "Want to start now?"

I slide her nightgown up and over her head, dropping it onto the floor. "This very second," I say.

She laughs against my neck, pulling me to her. "Just the answer I was hoping for."

And there's only one thing I know for sure.

Life is love. Beginning. Middle. End.

♪

Dear Reader

Dear Reader,

I would like to thank you for taking the time to read my story. There are so many wonderful books to choose from these days, and I am hugely appreciative that you chose mine.

Come check out my Facebook page for postings on books, dogs and things that make life good!

Wishing you many, many happy afternoons of reading pleasure.

All best,

Inglath

Get in Touch with Inglath Cooper

Email: inglathcooper@gmail.com
    Facebook – Inglath Cooper Books
    Instagram – inglath.cooper.books
    Pinterest – Inglath Cooper Books
    Twitter – InglathCooper

Books By Inglath Cooper

Swerve
The Heart That Breaks
My Italian Lover
Fences – Book Three – Smith Mountain Lake Series
Dragonfly Summer – Book Two – Smith Mountain Lake Series
Blue Wide Sky – Book One – Smith Mountain Lake Series
That Month in Tuscany
And Then You Loved Me
Down a Country Road
Good Guys Love Dogs
Truths and Roses
Nashville – Part Ten – Not Without You
Nashville – Book Nine – You, Me and a Palm Tree
Nashville – Book Eight – R U Serious
Nashville – Book Seven – Commit
Nashville – Book Six – Sweet Tea and Me
Nashville – Book Five – Amazed
Nashville – Book Four – Pleasure in the Rain
Nashville – Book Three – What We Feel
Nashville – Book Two – Hammer and a Song
Nashville – Book One – Ready to Reach
On Angel's Wings
A Gift of Grace
RITA® Award Winner John Riley's Girl
A Woman With Secrets
Unfinished Business
A Woman Like Annie
The Lost Daughter of Pigeon Hollow
A Year and a Day

About Inglath Cooper

RITA® Award-winning author Inglath Cooper was born in Virginia. She is a graduate of Virginia Tech with a degree in English. She fell in love with books as soon as she learned how to read. "My mom read to us before bed, and I think that's how I started to love stories. It was like a little mini-vacation we looked forward to every night before going to sleep. I think I eventually read most of the books in my elementary school library."

That love for books translated into a natural love for writing and a desire to create stories that other readers could get lost in, just as she had gotten lost in her favorite books. Her stories focus on the dynamics of relationships, those between a man and a woman, mother and daughter, sisters, friends. They most often take place in small Virginia towns very much like the one where she grew up and are peopled with characters who reflect those values and traditions.

"There's something about small-town life that's just part of who I am. I've had the desire to live in other places, wondered what it would be like to be a true Manhattanite, but the thing I know I would miss is the familiarity of faces everywhere I go. There's a lot to be said for going in the grocery store and seeing ten people you know!"

Inglath Cooper is an avid supporter of companion animal rescue and is a volunteer and donor for the Franklin County Humane Society. She and her family have fostered many dogs and cats that have gone on to be adopted by other families. "The rewards are endless. It's an eye-opening moment to realize that what one person throws away can fill another person's life with love and joy."

Follow Inglath on Facebook
at www.facebook.com/inglathcooperbooks

Made in the USA
Las Vegas, NV
13 October 2022

57189128R00085